DOVER · THRIFT · EDITIONS

The Trojan Women
and Hippolytus

EURIPIDES

Translated by

EDWARD P. COLERIDGE

DOVER PUBLICATIONS, INC.
Mineola, New York

Publisher's Note

The Trojan Women was first presented in 415 B.C. It is set at the end of the Trojan War, as the victorious Greeks set about the bloody final destruction of the city and its inhabitants. It depicts the anguish and despair of the surviving women (the men have all been killed) as they confront their fate of slavery and concubinage, and the cruelty and brutality of the victors—as well as their apparent moral shallowness and the triviality of their motives in waging the war. Aside from its unease at seeing heroic legends demystified, the Athenian audience would have been disturbed by the irony in the play's implicit commentary on current events. Less than a year earlier, during the ineffective Peace of Nikias that interrupted what we now call the Great or Second Peloponnesian War, Athens had "requested" the city of Melos to join its alliance (in truth a much-resented Athenian empire); the Melians preferred to remain neutral. The Athenians, arrogant in their power and confident of their moral rectitude, invaded the city, killed all the men and enslaved the women and children. Moreover, in an atmosphere of patriotic hysteria, Athens was just then preparing an expedition to conquer Sicily; Euripides opened his play with a prologue in which the city's protector goddess Athena arranged with Poseidon to destroy the Greeks as they returned home, because in their frenzied triumph they had thuggishly failed to respect her sanctuary or the person of her priestess Cassandra. (If this prologue was meant as a prediction, it was accurate; the Sicilian expedition was a complete disaster. The Athenian forces were destroyed, the great war was rekindled and Athenian power was eventually led to a defeat from which it never fully recovered.)

Hippolytus was first presented in 428 B.C. It concerns the dangers both of passion and of the struggle to control it by violating or thwarting normal desire. Hippolytus is the illegitimate son of Theseus, king of

iii

Athens, and the Amazon Antiope (or Hippolyte), whom Theseus had taken captive and raped. Perhaps as a result, Hippolytus has rejected love and sex, dedicating himself exclusively to an unnatural, immoderate pursuit of purity. He is devoted to the chaste goddess Artemis and completely neglects Aphrodite, goddess of erotic love. Aphrodite decides to punish Hippolytus by causing his stepmother Phaedra to conceive an overwhelming illicit passion for him, which she is driven nearly mad trying to resist. Hippolytus, told of Phaedra's secret desire by her old Nurse, angrily condemns her. Phaedra, thinking that Hippolytus will betray her to Theseus and unable to face her husband for guilt and shame, decides to revenge herself on Hippolytus by committing suicide and leaving a note for Theseus to find accusing Hippolytus of having ravished her. Hippolytus protests his innocence but honors his promise to the nurse to say nothing of what she has told him. Theseus banishes him and calls upon Poseidon to destroy him.

EURIPIDES (c.485–c.406 B.C) was one of the three great Athenian tragic dramatists of the fifth century BC. Though not as successful in winning prizes as those of his great contemporaries Aeschylus and Sophocles, his plays were popular and became the most frequently performed in later centuries, when the others' works were seen as outdated and archaic. Euripides' plays led to the development of the New Comedy of the fourth century, considered to be the beginning of the European dramatic tradition that lives to this day.

Euripides' work shows the influence of the Sophists, relatively pragmatic and open-minded thinkers much derided by conservatives of the time who clung to the more hierarchical, essentialist beliefs about human nature associated with traditional aristocratic rule. His characters, taken from the Homeric and post-Homeric myths and legends, are rendered with greater psychological realism, within theatrical convention, than those of his contemporaries, making him seem comparatively modern—though it is wise to remember, in the words of one modern historian, "how remote, mysterious and unknown the tragic drama of the ancient Athenians must be for us; only the words of the dramas remain. . . . Their past and present will always be shrouded for us."*

---

*Charles Rowan Beye, *Ancient Greek Literature and Society*.

THE TROJAN WOMEN

DRAMATIS PERSONÆ

POSEIDON.

ATHENA.

HECUBA.

CHORUS OF CAPTIVE TROJAN WOMEN.

TALTHYBIUS.

CASSANDRA.

ANDROMACHE.

MENELAUS.

HELEN.

SCENE. —Before Agamemnon's Tent in the Camp near Troy.

THE TROJAN WOMEN

POS. Lo! from the depths of salt Ægean floods I, Poseidon, come, where choirs of Nereids trip in the mazes of the graceful dance; for since the day that Phœbus and myself with measurement exact set towers of stone about this land of Troy and ringed it round, never from my heart hath passed away a kindly feeling for my Phrygian town, which now is smouldering and o'erthrown, a prey to Argive prowess. For, from his home beneath Parnassus, Phocian Epeus, aided by the craft of Pallas, framed a horse to bear within its womb an armed host, and sent it within the battlements, fraught with death; whence in days to come men shall tell of "The wooden horse," with its hidden load of warriors. Groves forsaken stand and temples of the gods run down with blood, and at the altar's very base, before the god who watched his home, lies Priam dead. While to Achæan ships great store of gold and Phrygian spoils are being conveyed, and they who came against this town, those sons of Hellas, only wait a favouring breeze to follow in their wake, that after ten long years they may with joy behold their wives and children. Vanquished by Hera, Argive goddess, and by Athena, who helped to ruin Phrygia, I am leaving Ilium, that famous town, and the altars that I love; for when drear desolation seizes on a town, the worship of the gods decays and tends to lose respect. Scamander's banks re-echo long and loud the screams of captive maids, as they by lot receive their masters. Arcadia taketh some, and some the folk of Thessaly; others are assigned to Theseus' sons, the Athenian chiefs. And such of the Trojan dames as are not portioned out, are in these tents, set apart for the leaders of the host; and with them Spartan Helen, daughter of Tyndarus, justly counted among the captives. And wouldst thou see that queen of misery, Hecuba, thou canst; for there she lies before the gates, weeping many a bitter tear for many a tribulation; for at Achilles' tomb,—though she knows not this,—her daughter Polyxena has died most piteously; likewise is Priam dead, and her

3

children too; Cassandra, whom the king Apollo left to be a virgin, frenzied maid, hath Agamemnon, in contempt of the god's ordinance and of piety, forced to a dishonoured wedlock. Farewell, O city prosperous once! farewell, ye ramparts of hewn stone! had not Pallas, daughter of Zeus, decreed thy ruin, thou wert standing firmly still.

ATH. May I address the mighty god whom Heaven reveres and who to my own sire is very nigh in blood, laying aside our former enmity?

POS. Thou mayst; for o'er the soul the ties of kin exert no feeble spell, great queen Athena.

ATH. For thy forgiving mood my thanks! Somewhat have I to impart affecting both thyself and me, O king.

POS. Bringst thou fresh tidings from some god, from Zeus, or from some lesser power?

ATH. From none of these; but on behalf of Troy, whose soil we tread, am I come to seek thy mighty aid, to make it one with mine.

POS. What! hast thou laid thy former hate aside to take compassion on the town now that it is burnt to ashes?

ATH. First go back to the former point; wilt thou make common cause with me in the scheme I purpose?

POS. Ay surely; but I would fain learn thy wishes, whether thou art come to help Achæans or Phrygians.

ATH. I wish to give my former foes, the Trojans, joy, and on the Achæan host impose a return that they will rue.

POS. Why leap'st thou thus from mood to mood? Thy love and hate both go too far, on whomsoever centred.

ATH. Dost not know the insult done to me and to the shrine I love?

POS. Surely, in the hour that Aias tore Cassandra thence.

ATH. Yea, and the Achæans did naught, said naught to him.

POS. And yet 'twas by thy mighty aid they sacked Ilium.

ATH. For which cause I would join with thee to work their bane.

POS. My powers are ready at thy will. What is thy intent?

ATH. A returning fraught with woe will I impose on them.

POS. While yet they stay on shore, or as they cross the briny deep?

ATH. When they have set sail from Ilium for their homes. On them will Zeus also send his rain and fearful hail, and inky tempests from the sky; yea, and he promises to grant me his levin-bolts to hurl on the Achæans and fire their ships. And do thou, for thy part, make the Ægean strait to roar with mighty billows and whirlpools, and fill Eubœa's hollow bay with corpses, that Achæans may learn henceforth to reverence my temples and regard all other deities.

POS. So shall it be, for the boon thou cravest needs but few words. I will vex the broad Ægean sea; and the beach of Myconus and the reefs round Delos, Scyros and Lemnos too, and the cliffs of Caphareus shall be strown with many a corpse. Mount thou to Olympus, and taking from thy father's hand his lightning bolts, keep careful watch against the hour when Argos' host lets slip its cables. A fool is he who sacks the towns of men, with shrines and tombs, the dead man's hallowed home, for at the last he makes a desert round himself, and dies.

HEC. Lift thy head, unhappy lady, from the ground; thy neck upraise; this is Troy no more, no longer am I queen in Ilium. Though fortune change, endure thy lot; sail with the stream, and follow fortune's tack, steer not thy barque of life against the tide, since chance must guide thy course. Ah me! ah me! What else but tears is now my hapless lot, whose country, children, husband, all are lost? Ah! the high-blown pride of ancestors! how cabined now! how brought to nothing after all! What woe must I suppress, or what declare? What plaintive dirge shall I awake? Ah, woe is me! the anguish I suffer lying here stretched upon this pallet hard! O my head, my temples, my side! Ah! could I but turn over, and lie now on this, now on that, to rest my back and spine, while ceaselessly my tearful wail ascends. For e'en this is music to the wretched, to chant their cheerless dirge of sorrow.

Ye swift-prowed ships, rowed to sacred Ilium o'er the deep dark sea, past the fair havens of Hellas, to the flute's ill-omened music and the dulcet voice of pipes, even to the bays of Troyland (alack the day!), wherein ye tied your hawsers, twisted handiwork from Egypt, in quest of that hateful wife of Menelaus, who brought disgrace on Castor, and on Eurotas foul reproach; murderess she of Priam, sire of fifty children, the cause why I, the hapless Hecuba, have wrecked my life upon this troublous strand. Oh that I should sit here o'er against the tent of Agamemnon! Forth from my home to slavery they hale my aged frame, while from my head in piteous wise the hair is shorn for grief. Ah! hapless wives of those mail-clad sons of Troy! Ah! poor maidens, luckless brides, come weep, for Ilium is now but a smouldering ruin; and I, like some mother-bird that o'er her fledgelings screams, will begin the strain; how different from that song I sang to the gods in days long past, as I leaned on Priam's staff, and beat with my foot in Phrygian time to lead the dance!

1ST HALF-CHO. O Hecuba! why these cries, these piercing shrieks? What mean thy words? For I heard thy piteous wail echo through the building, and a pang of terror shoots through each captive

Trojan's breast, as pent within these walls thy mourn their slavish lot.

HEC.　My child, e'en now the hands of Argive rowers are busy at their ships.

1ST HALF-CHO.　Ah, woe is me! what is their intent? Will they really bear me hence in sorrow from my country in their fleet?

HEC.　I know not, though I guess our doom.

1ST HALF-CHO.　O misery! woe to us Trojan dames, soon to hear the order given, "Come forth from the house; the Argives are preparing to return."

HEC.　Oh! do not bid the wild Cassandra leave her chamber, the frantic prophetess, for Argives to insult, nor to my griefs add yet another. Woe to thee, ill-fated Troy, thy sun is set; and woe to thy unhappy children, quick and dead alike, who are leaving thee behind!

2ND HALF-CHO.　With trembling step, alas! I leave this tent of Agamemnon to learn of thee, my royal mistress, whether the Argives have resolved to take my wretched life, whether the sailors at the prow are making ready to ply their oars.

HEC.　My child, a fearful dread seized on my wakeful heart and sent me hither.

2ND HALF-CHO.　Hath a herald from the Danai already come? To whom am I, poor captive, given as a slave?

HEC.　Thou art not far from being allotted now.

2ND HALF-CHO.　Woe worth the day! What Argive or Phthiotian chief will bear me far from Troy, alas! unto his home, or haply to some island fastness?

HEC.　Ah me! ah me! Whose slave shall I become in my old age? in what far clime? a poor old drone, the wretched copy of a corpse, set to keep the gate or tend their children, I who once held royal rank in Troy.

CHO.　Woe, woe is thee! What piteous dirge wilt thou devise to mourn the outrage done thee? No more through Ida's looms shall I ply the shuttle to and fro. I look my last and latest on my children's bodies; henceforth shall I endure surpassing misery; it may be as the unwilling bride of some Hellene (perish the night and fortune that brings me to this!); it may be as a wretched slave I from Peirene's sacred fount shall draw their store of water.

　　　Oh! be it ours to come to Theseus' famous realm, a land of joy! Never, never let me see Eurotas' swirling tide, hateful home of Helen, there to meet and be the slave of Menelaus, whose hand laid Troyland waste! Yon holy land by Peneus fed, nestling in all its beauty at Olympus' foot, is said, so have I heard, to be a very

granary of wealth and teeming fruitage; next to the sacred soil of
Theseus, I could wish to reach that land. They tell me too
Hephæstus' home, beneath the shadow of Ætna, fronting
Phœnicia, the mother of Sicilian hills, is famous for the crowns it
gives to worth. Or may I find a home on that shore which lieth
very nigh Ionia's sea, a land by Crathis watered, lovely stream, that
dyes the hair an auburn tint, feeding with its holy waves and making glad therewith the home of heroes good and true.

But mark! a herald from the host of Danai, with store of fresh
proclamations, comes hasting hither. What is his errand? what
saith he? List, for we are slaves to Dorian lords henceforth.

TAL.   Hecuba, thou knowest me from my many journeys to and fro as
herald 'twixt the Achæan host and Troy; no stranger I to thee, lady,
even aforetime, I Talthybius, now sent with a fresh message.

HEC.   Ah, kind friends, 'tis come! what I so long have dreaded.

TAL.   The lot has decided your fates already, if that was what you
feared.

HEC.   Ah me! What city didst thou say, Thessalian, Phthian, or
Cadmean?

TAL.   Each warrior took his prize in turn; ye were not all at once
assigned.

HEC.   To whom hath the lot assigned us severally? Which of us Trojan
dames doth a happy fortune await?

TAL.   I know, but ask thy questions separately, not all at once.

HEC.   Then tell me, whose prize is my daughter, hapless Cassandra?

TAL.   King Agamemnon hath chosen her out for himself.

HEC.   To be the slave-girl of his Spartan wife? Ah me!

TAL.   Nay, to share with him his stealthy love.

HEC.   What! Phœbus' virgin-priestess, to whom the god with golden
locks granted the boon of maidenhood?

TAL.   The dart of love hath pierced his heart, love for the frenzied
maid.

HEC.   Daughter, cast from thee the sacred keys, and from thy body
tear the holy wreaths that drape thee in their folds.

TAL.   Why! is it not an honour high that she should win our
monarch's love?

HEC.   What have ye done to her whom late ye took from me,—my
child?

TAL.   Dost mean Polyxena, or whom dost thou inquire about?

HEC.   To whom hath the lot assigned her?

TAL.   To minister at Achilles' tomb hath been appointed her.

HEC.   Woe is me! I the mother of a dead man's slave! What custom,
what ordinance is this amongst Hellenes, good sir?

TAL. Count thy daughter happy: 'tis well with her.

HEC. What wild words are these? say, is she still alive?

TAL. Her fate is one that sets her free from trouble.

HEC. And what of mail-clad Hector's wife, sad Andromache? declare her fate.

TAL. She too was a chosen prize; Achilles' son did take her.

HEC. As for me whose hair is white with age, who need to hold a staff to be to me a third foot, whose servant am I to be?

TAL. Odysseus, king of Ithaca, hath taken thee to be his slave.

HEC. O God! Now smite the close-shorn head! tear your cheeks with your nails. God help me! I have fallen as a slave to a treacherous foe I hate, a monster of lawlessness, one that by his double tongue hath turned against us all that once was friendly in his camp, changing this for that and that for this again. Oh weep for me, ye Trojan dames! Undone! undone and lost! ah woe! a victim to a most unhappy lot!

CHO. Thy fate, royal mistress, now thou knowest; but for me, what Hellene or Achæan is master of my destiny?

TAL. Ho, servants! haste and bring Cassandra forth to me here, that I may place her in our captain's hands, and then conduct to the rest of the chiefs the captives each hath had assigned. Ha! what is the blaze of torches there within? What do these Trojan dames? Are they firing the chambers, because they must leave this land and be carried away to Argos? Are they setting themselves aflame in their longing for death? Of a truth the free bear their troubles in cases like this with a stiff neck. Ho, there! open! lest their deed, which suits them well but finds small favour with the Achæans, bring blame on me.

HEC. 'Tis not that they are setting aught ablaze, but my child Cassandra, frenzied maid, comes rushing wildly hither.

CAS. Bring the light, uplift and show its flame! I am doing the god's service, see! see! making his shrine to glow with tapers bright. O Hymen, king of marriage! blest is the bridegroom; blest am I also, the maiden soon to wed a princely lord in Argos. Hail Hymen, king of marriage! Since thou, my mother, art ever busied with tears and lamentations in thy mourning for my father's death and for our country dear, I at my own nuptials am making this torch to blaze and show its light, in thy honour, O Hymen, king of marriage! Grant thy light too, Hecate, at the maiden's wedding, as the custom is. Nimbly lift the foot aloft, lead on the dance, with cries of joy, as if to greet my father's happy fate. To dance I hold a sacred duty; come, Phœbus, lead the way, for 'tis in thy temple mid thy bay-trees that I minister. Hail Hymen, god of marriage!

Hymen, hail! Come, mother mine, and join the dance, link thy steps with me, and circle in the gladsome measure, now here, now there. Salute the bride on her wedding-day with hymns and cries of joy. Come, ye maids of Phrygia in raiment fair, sing my marriage with the husband fate ordains that I should wed.

CHO.   Hold the frantic maiden, royal mistress mine, lest with nimble foot she rush to the Argive army.

HEC.   Thou god of fire, 'tis thine to light the bridal torch for men, but piteous is the flame thou kindlest here, beyond my blackest bodings. Ah, my child! how little did I ever dream that such would be thy marriage, a captive, and of Argos too! Give up the torch to me; thou dost not bear its blaze aright in thy wild frantic course, nor have thy afflictions left thee in thy sober senses, but still art thou as frantic as before. Take in those torches, Trojan friends, and for her wedding madrigals weep your tears instead.

CAS.   O mother, crown my head with victor's wreaths; rejoice in my royal match; lead me to my lord; nay, if thou find me loth at all, thrust me there by force; for if Loxias be indeed a prophet, Agamemnon, that famous king of the Achæans, will find in me a bride more fraught with woe to him than Helen. For I will slay him and lay waste his home to avenge my father's and my brethren's death. But of the deed itself I will not speak; nor will I tell of that axe which shall sever my neck and the necks of others, or of the conflict ending in a mother's death, which my marriage shall cause, nor of the overthrow of Atreus' house; but I, for all my frenzy, will so far rise above my frantic fit, that I will prove this city happier far than those Achæans, who for the sake of one woman and one man's love of her have lost a countless host in seeking Helen. Their captain too, whom men call wise, hath lost for what he hated most what most he prized, yielding to his brother for a woman's sake,—and she a willing prize whom no man forced,—the joy he had of his own children in his home. For from the day that they did land upon Scamander's strand, their doom began, not for loss of stolen frontier nor yet for fatherland with frowning towers; whomso Ares slew, those never saw their babes again, nor were they shrouded for the tomb by hand of wife, but in a foreign land they lie. At home the case was still the same; wives were dying widows, parents were left childless in their homes, having reared their sons for others, and none is left to make libations of blood upon the ground before their tombs. Truly to such praise as this their host can make an ample claim. 'Tis better to pass their shame in silence by, nor be mine the Muse to tell that evil tale. But the Trojans were dying, first for their fatherland, fairest fame to win; whomso the sword laid low, all these found friends to bear their bodies home and were laid to rest in the bosom of their native land, their funeral rites all duly paid by duteous hands. And all such Phrygians as escaped the warrior's death lived ever day by day with wife and children by them,—joys the Achæans had left behind. As for Hector and his griefs, prithee hear how stands the case; he is dead and gone, but still his fame remains as bravest of the brave, and this was a result of the Achæans' coming; for had they remained at home, his worth would have gone unnoticed. So too with Paris, he married the daughter of Zeus, whereas, had he never done so, the alliance he made in his family would have been forgotten. Whoso is wise should fly from making war; but if he be brought to this pass, a noble death will crown his city with glory, a coward's end with shame. Wherefore, mother mine, thou shouldst not pity thy country or my spousal, for this my marriage will destroy those whom thou and I most hate.

CHO. How sweetly at thy own sad lot thou smilest, chanting a strain, which, spite of thee, may prove thee wrong!

TAL. Had not Apollo turned thy wits astray, thou shouldst not for nothing have sent my chiefs with such ominous predictions forth on their way. But, after all, these lofty minds, reputed wise, are nothing better than those that are held as naught. For that mighty king of all Hellas, own son of Atreus, has yielded to a passion for this mad maiden of all others; though I am poor enough, yet would I ne'er have chosen such a wife as this. As for thee, since thy senses are not whole, I give thy taunts 'gainst Argos and thy praise of Troy to the winds to carry away. Follow me now to the ships to grace the wedding of our chief. And thou too follow, whensoe'er the son of Laertes demands thy presence, for thou wilt serve a mistress most discreet, as all declare who came to Ilium.

CAS. A clever fellow this menial! Why is it heralds hold the name they do? All men unite in hating with one common hate the servants who attend on kings or governments. Thou sayest my mother shall come to the halls of Odysseus; where then be Apollo's words, so clear to me in their interpretation, which declare that here she shall die? What else remains, I will not taunt her with. Little knows he, the luckless wight, the sufferings that await him; or how these ills I and my Phrygians endure shall one day seem to him precious as gold. For beyond the ten long years spent at Troy he shall drag out other ten and then come to his country all alone, by the route where fell Charybdis lurks in a narrow channel 'twixt the rocks; past Cyclops the savage shepherd, and Ligurian Circe that turneth men to swine; shipwrecked oft upon the salt sea-wave; fain to eat the lotus, and the sacred cattle of the sun, whose flesh shall utter in the days to come a human voice, fraught with misery to Odysseus. But to briefly end this history, he shall descend alive to Hades, and, though he 'scape the waters' flood, yet shall he find a thousand troubles in his home when he arrives. Enough! why do I recount the troubles of Odysseus? Lead on, that I forthwith may wed my husband for his home in Hades' halls. Base thou art, and basely shalt thou be buried, in the dead of night when day is done, thou captain of that host of Danai, who thinkest so proudly of thy fortune! Yea, and my corpse cast forth in nakedness shall the rocky chasm with its flood of wintry waters give to wild beasts to make their meal upon, hard by my husband's tomb, me the handmaid of Apollo. Farewell, ye garlands of that god most dear to me! farewell, ye mystic symbols! I here resign your feasts, my joy in days gone by. Go, I tear ye from my body, that, while yet mine honour is intact, I may give them to the rushing winds to waft to thee, my prince of prophecy! Where is yon general's ship? Whither must I go to take my place thereon? Lose no further time in watching for a favouring breeze to fill thy sails, doomed as thou art to carry from this land one of the three avenging spirits. Fare thee well, mother mine! dry thy tears, O country dear! yet a little while, my brothers sleeping in the tomb and my own father true, and ye shall welcome me; yet shall victory crown my advent 'mongst the dead, when I have overthrown the home of our destroyers, the house of the sons of Atreus.

CHO. Ye guardians of the grey-haired Hecuba, see how your mistress is sinking speechless to the ground! Take hold of her! will ye let her fall, ye worthless slaves? lift up again, from where it lies, her silvered head.

HEC. Leave me lying where I fell, my maidens—unwelcome service grows not welcome ever—my sufferings now, my troubles past, afflictions yet to come, all claim this lowly posture. Gods of heaven! small help I find in calling such allies, yet is there something in the form of invoking heaven, whenso we fall on evil days. First will I descant upon my former blessings; so shall I inspire the greater pity for my present woes. Born to royal estate and wedded to a royal lord, I was the mother of a race of gallant sons; no mere ciphers they, but Phrygia's chiefest pride, children such as no Trojan or Hellenic or barbarian mother ever had to boast. All these have I seen slain by the spear of Hellas, and at their tombs have I shorn off my hair; with these my eyes I saw their sire, my Priam, butchered on his own hearth, and my city captured, nor did others bring this bitter news to me. The maidens I brought up to see chosen for some marriage high, for strangers have I reared them, and seen them snatched away. Nevermore can I hope to be seen by them, nor shall my eyes behold them ever in the days to come. And last, to crown my misery, shall I be brought to Hellas, a slave in my old age. And there the tasks that least befit the evening of my life will they impose on me, to watch their gates and keep the keys, me Hector's mother, or bake their bread, and on the ground instead of my royal bed lay down my shrunken limbs, with tattered rags about my wasted frame, a shameful garb for those who once were prosperous. Ah, woe is me! and this is what I bear and am to bear for one weak woman's wooing! O my daughter, O Cassandra! whom gods have summoned to their frenzied train, how cruel the lot that ends thy virgin days! And thou, Polyxena! my child of sorrow, where, oh! where art thou? None of all the many sons and daughters I have born comes to aid a wretched mother. Why then raise me up? What hope is left us? Guide me, who erst trod so daintily the streets of Troy, but now am but a slave, to a bed upon the ground, nigh some rocky ridge, that thence I may cast me down and perish, after I have wasted my body with weeping. Of all the prosperous crowd, count none a happy man before he die.

CHO.   Sing me, Muse, a tale of Troy, a funeral dirge in strains unheard as yet, with tears the while; for now will I uplift for Troy a piteous chant, telling how I met my doom and fell a wretched captive to the Argives by reason of a four-footed beast that moved on wheels, in the hour that Achæa's sons left at our gates that horse, loud rumbling on its way, with its trappings of gold and its freight of warriors; and our folk cried out as they stood upon the rocky citadel, "Up now ye whose toil is o'er, and drag this sacred image to the shrine of the Zeus-born maiden, goddess of our Ilium!" Forth from his house came every youth and every grey-head too; and with songs of joy they took the fatal snare within. Then hastened all the race of Phrygia to the gates, to make the goddess a present of an Argive band ambushed in the polished mountain-pine, Dardania's ruin, a welcome gift to be to her, the virgin queen of deathless steeds; and with nooses of cord they dragged it, as it had been a ship's dark hull, to the stone-built fane of the goddess Pallas, and set it on that floor so soon to drink our country's blood. But, as they laboured and made merry, came on the pitchy night; loud the Libyan flute was sounding, and Phrygian songs awoke, while maidens beat the ground with airy foot, uplifting their gladsome song; and in the halls a blaze of torchlight shed its flickering shadows on sleeping eyes. In that hour around the house was I singing as I danced to that maiden of the hills, the child of Zeus; when lo! there rang along the town a cry of death which filled the homes of Troy, and little babes in terror clung about their mothers' skirts, as forth from their ambush came the warrior-band, the handiwork of maiden Pallas. Anon the altars ran with Phrygian blood, and desolation reigned o'er every bed where young men lay beheaded, a glorious crown for Hellas won, ay, for her, the nurse of youth, but for our Phrygian fatherland a bitter grief. Look, Hecuba! dost see Andromache advancing hither on a foreign car? and with her, clasped to her throbbing breast, is her dear Astyanax, Hector's child.

HEC. Whither art thou borne, unhappy wife, mounted on that car, side by side with Hector's brazen arms and Phrygian spoils of war, with which Achilles' son will deck the shrines of Phthia on his return from Troy?

AND. My Achæan masters drag me hence.

HEC. Woe is thee!

AND. Why dost thou in note of woe utter the dirge that is mine?

HEC. Ah me!

AND. For these sorrows.

HEC. O Zeus!

AND. And for this calamity.

HEC. O my children!

AND. Our day is past.

HEC. Joy is fled, and Troy o'erthrown.

AND. Woe is me!

HEC. Dead too all my gallant sons!

AND. Alack and well-a-day!

HEC. Ah me for my—

AND. Misery!

HEC. Piteous the fate

AND. Of our city,

HEC. Smouldering in the smoke.

AND. Come, my husband, come to me!

HEC. Ah hapless wife! thou callest on my son who lieth in the tomb.

AND. Thy wife's defender, come!

HEC. Do thou, who erst didst make the Achæans grieve, eldest of the sons I bare to Priam in the days gone by, take me to thy rest in Hades' halls!

AND. Bitter are these regrets, unhappy mother, bitter these woes to bear; our city ruined, and sorrow evermore to sorrow added, through the will of angry heaven, since the day that son of thine escaped his doom, he that for a bride accursed brought destruction on the Trojan citadel. There lie the gory corpses of the slain by the shrine of Pallas for vultures to carry off; and Troy is come to slavery's yoke.

HEC.   O my country, O unhappy land, I weep for thee now left behind; now dost thou behold thy piteous end; and thee, my house, I weep, wherein I suffered travail. O my children! reft of her city as your mother is, she now is losing you. Oh, what mourning and what sorrow! oh, what endless streams of tears in our houses! The dead alone forget their griefs and never shed a tear.

CHO.   What sweet relief to sufferers 'tis to weep, to mourn, lament, and chant the dirge that tells of grief!

AND.   Dost thou see this, mother of that Hector, who once laid low in battle many a son of Argos?

HEC.   I see that it is heaven's way to exalt what men accounted naught, and ruin what they most esteemed.

AND.   Hence with my child as booty am I borne; the noble are to slavery brought—a bitter, bitter change.

HEC.   This is necessity's grim law; it was but now Cassandra was torn with brutal violence from my arms.

AND.   Alas, alas! it seems a second Aias hath appeared to wrong thy daughter; but there be other ills for thee.

HEC.   Ay, beyond all count or measure are my sorrows; evil vies with evil in the struggle to be first.

AND.   Thy daughter Polyxena is dead, slain at Achilles' tomb, an offering to his lifeless corpse.

HEC.   O woe is me! This is that riddle Talthybius long since told me, a truth obscurely uttered.

AND.   I saw her with mine eyes; so I alighted from the chariot, and covered her corpse with a mantle, and smote upon my breast.

HEC.   Alas! my child, for thy unhallowed sacrifice! and yet again, ah me! for this thy shameful death!

AND.   Her death was even as it was, and yet that death of hers was after all a happier fate than this my life.

HEC.   Death and life are not the same, my child; the one is annihilation, the other keeps a place for hope.

AND.   Hear, O mother of children! give ear to what I urge so well, that I may cheer my drooping spirit. 'Tis all one, I say, ne'er to have been born and to be dead, and better far is death than life with misery. For the dead feel no sorrow any more and know no grief; but he who has known prosperity and has fallen on evil days feels his spirit straying from the scene of former joys. Now that child of thine is dead as though she ne'er had seen the light, and little she recks of her calamity; whereas I, who aimed at a fair repute, though I won a higher lot than most, yet missed my luck in life.

For all that stamps the wife a woman chaste, I strove to do in Hector's home. In the first place, whether there is a slur upon a woman, or whether there is not, the very fact of her not staying at home brings in its train an evil name; therefore I gave up any wish to do so, and abode ever within my house, nor would I admit the clever gossip women love, but conscious of a heart that told an honest tale I was content therewith. And ever would I keep a silent tongue and modest eye before my lord; and well I knew where I might rule my lord, and where 'twas best to yield to him; the fame whereof hath reached the Achæan host, and proved my ruin; for when I was taken captive, Achilles' son would have me as his wife, and I must serve in the house of murderers. And if I set aside my love for Hector, and ope my heart to this new lord, I shall appear a traitress to the dead, while, if I hate him, I shall incur my master's displeasure. And yet they say a single night removes a woman's dislike for her husband; nay, I do hate the woman who, when she hath lost her former lord, transfers her love by marrying another. Not e'en the horse, if from his fellow torn, will cheerfully draw the yoke; and yet the brutes have neither speech nor sense to help them, and are by nature man's inferiors. O Hector mine! in thee I found a husband amply dowered with wisdom, noble birth and fortune, a brave man and a mighty; whilst thou didst take me from my father's house a spotless bride, thyself the first to make this maiden wife. But now death hath claimed thee, and I to Hellas am soon to sail, a captive doomed to wear the yoke of slavery. Hath not then the dead Polyxena, for whom thou wailest, less evil to bear than I? I have not so much as hope, the last resource of every human heart, nor do I beguile myself with dreams of future bliss, the very thought whereof is sweet.

CHO.   Thou art in the self-same plight as I; thy lamentations for thyself remind me of my own sad case.

HEC.   I never yet have set foot on a ship's deck, though I have seen such things in pictures and know of them from hearsay. Now sailors, if there come a storm of moderate force, are all eagerness to save themselves by toil; one at the tiller stands, another sets himself to work the sheets, a third meantime is baling out the ship; but if tempestuous waves arise to overwhelm them, they yield to fortune and commit themselves to the driving billows. Even so I, by reason of my countless troubles, am dumb and forbear to say a word; for Heaven with its surge of misery is too strong for me. Cease, Oh cease, my darling child, to speak of Hector's fate; no tears of thine can save him; honour thy present lord, offering thy sweet nature as the bait to win him. If thou do this, thou wilt cheer thy friends as well as thyself, and thou shalt rear my Hector's child to lend stout aid to Ilium, that so thy children in the after-time may build her up again, and our city yet be stablished. But lo! our talk must take a different turn; who is this Achæan menial I see coming hither, sent to tell us of some new design?

TAL. Oh hate me not, thou that erst wert Hector's wife, the bravest of the Phrygians! for my tongue would fain not tell that which the Danai and sons of Pelops both command.

AND. What is it? Thy prelude bodeth evil news.

TAL. 'Tis decreed thy son is—how can I tell my news?

AND. Surely not to have a different master from me?

TAL. None of all Achæa's chiefs shall ever lord it over him.

AND. Is it their will to leave him here, a remnant yet of Phrygia's race?

TAL. I know no words to break the sorrow lightly to thee.

AND. I thank thee for thy consideration, unless indeed thou hast good news to tell.

TAL. They mean to slay thy son; there is my hateful message to thee.

AND. O God! this is worse tidings than my forced marriage.

TAL. So spake Odysseus to the assembled Hellenes, and his word prevails.

AND. Oh once again ah me! there is no measure in the woes I bear.

TAL. He said they should not rear so brave a father's son.

AND. May such counsels yet prevail about children of his!

TAL. From Troy's battlements he must be thrown. Let it be even so, and thou wilt show more wisdom; cling not to him, but bear thy sorrows with heroic heart, nor in thy weakness deem that thou art strong. For nowhere hast thou any help; consider this thou must; thy husband and thy city are no more, so thou art in our power, and I alone am match enough for one weak woman; wherefore I would not see thee bent on strife, or any course to bring thee shame or hate, nor would I hear thee rashly curse the Achæans. For if thou say aught whereat the host grow wroth, this child will find no burial nor pity either. But if thou hold thy peace and with composure take thy fate, thou wilt not leave his corpse unburied, and thyself wilt find more favour with the Achæans.

AND. My child! my own sweet babe and priceless treasure! thy death the foe demands, and thou must leave thy wretched mother. That which saves the lives of others, proves thy destruction, even thy sire's nobility; to thee thy father's valiancy has proved no boon. O the woful wedding rites, that brought me erst to Hector's home, hoping to be the mother of a son that should rule o'er Asia's fruitful fields instead of serving as a victim to the sons of Danaus! Dost weep, my babe? dost know thy hapless fate? Why clutch me with thy hands and to my garment cling, nestling like a tender chick beneath my wing? Hector will not rise again and come gripping his famous spear to bring thee salvation; no kinsman of thy sire appears, nor might of Phrygian hosts; one awful headlong leap from the dizzy height and thou wilt dash out thy life with none to pity thee! Oh to clasp thy tender limbs, a mother's fondest joy! Oh to breathe thy fragrant breath! In vain it seems these breasts did suckle thee, wrapped in thy swaddling-clothes; all for naught I used to toil and wore myself away! Kiss thy mother now for the last time, nestle to her that bare thee, twine thy arms about my neck and join thy lips to mine! O ye Hellenes, cunning to devise new forms of cruelty, why slay this child who never wronged any? Thou daughter of Tyndarus, thou art no child of Zeus, but sprung, I trow, of many a sire, first of some evil demon, next of Envy, then of Murder and of Death, and every horror that the earth begets. That Zeus was never sire of thine I boldly do assert, bane as thou hast been to many a Hellene and barbarian too. Destruction catch thee! Those fair eyes of thine have brought a shameful ruin on the fields of glorious Troy. Take the babe and bear him hence, hurl him down if so ye list, then feast upon his flesh! 'Tis heaven's high will we perish, and I cannot ward the deadly stroke from my child. Hide me and my misery; cast me into the ship's hold; for 'tis to a fair wedding I am going, now that I have lost my child!

CHO. Unhappy Troy! thy thousands thou hast lost for one woman's sake and her accursed wooing.

TAL. Come, child, leave fond embracing of thy woful mother, and mount the high coronal of thy ancestral towers, there to draw thy parting breath, as is ordained. Take him hence. His should the duty be to do such herald's work, whose heart knows no pity and who loveth ruthlessness more than my soul doth.

[*Exeunt* ANDROMACHE *and* TALTHYBIUS *with* ASTYANAX.]

HEC. O child, son of my hapless boy, an unjust fate robs me and thy mother of thy life. How is it with me? What can I do for thee, my luckless babe? for thee I smite upon my head and beat my breast, my only gift; for that alone is in my power. Woe for my city! woe for thee! Is not our cup full? What is wanting now to our utter and immediate ruin?

CHO. O Telamon, King of Salamis, the feeding-ground of bees, who hast thy home in a sea-girt isle that lieth nigh the holy hills where first Athena made the grey olive-branch to appear, a crown for heavenly heads and a glory unto happy Athens, thou didst come in knightly brotherhood with that great archer, Alcmena's son, to

sack our city Ilium, in days gone by, [on thy advent from Hellas,]
what time he led the chosen flower of Hellas, vexed for the steeds
denied him, and at the fair stream of Simois he stayed his sea-
borne ship and fastened cables to the stern, and forth therefrom he
took the bow his hand could deftly shoot, to be the doom of
Laomedon; and with the ruddy breath of fire he wasted the ma-
sonry squared by Phœbus' line and chisel, and sacked the land of
Troy; so twice in two attacks hath the blood-stained spear destroyed Dardania's walls.

In vain, it seems, thou Phrygian boy, pacing with dainty step
amid thy golden chalices, dost thou fill high the cup of Zeus, a service passing fair; seeing that the land of thy birth is being con-
sumed by fire. The shore re-echoes to our cries; and, as a bird be-
wails its young, so we bewail our husbands or our children, or our
grey-haired mothers. The dew-fed springs where thou didst bathe,
the course where thou didst train, are now no more; but thou beside the throne of Zeus art sitting with a calm, sweet smile upon
thy fair young face, while the spear of Hellas lays the land of Priam
waste. Ah! Love, Love, who once didst seek these Dardan halls,
deep-seated in the hearts of heavenly gods, how high didst thou
make Troy to tower in those days, allying her with deities! But I
will cease to urge reproaches against Zeus; for white-winged
dawn, whose light to man is dear, turned a baleful eye upon our
land and watched the ruin of our citadel, though she had within
her bridal bower a husband from this land, whom on a day a car
of gold and spangled stars caught up and carried thither, great
source of hope to his native country; but all the love the gods once
had for Troy is passed away.

MEN.   Hail! thou radiant orb by whose fair light I now shall capture
her that was my wife, e'en Helen; for I am that Menelaus, who
hath toiled so hard, I and Achæa's host. To Troy I came, not so
much as men suppose to take this woman, but to punish him who
from my house stole my wife, traitor to my hospitality. But he, by
heaven's will, hath paid the penalty, ruined, and his country too,
by the spear of Hellas. And I am come to bear that Spartan woman
hence—wife I have no mind to call her, though she once was
mine; for now she is but one among the other Trojan dames who
share these tents as captives. For they,—the very men who toiled
to take her with the spear,—have granted her to me to slay, or, if
I will, to spare and carry back with me to Argos. Now my purpose
is not to put her to death in Troy, but to carry her to Hellas in my
sea-borne ship, and then surrender her to death, a recompense to
all whose friends were slain in Ilium. Ho! my trusty men, enter the

tent, and drag her out to me by her hair with many a murder foul; and when a favouring breeze shall blow, to Hellas will we convey her.

HEC. O thou that dost support the earth and restest thereupon, whosoe'er thou art, a riddle past our ken! be thou Zeus, or natural necessity, or man's intellect, to thee I pray; for, though thou treadest o'er a noiseless path, all thy dealings with mankind are by justice guided.

MEN. How now? Strange the prayer thou offerest unto heaven!

HEC. I thank thee, Menelaus, if thou wilt slay that wife of thine. Yet shun the sight of her, lest she smite thee with regret. For she ensnares the eyes of men, o'erthrows their towns, and burns their houses, so potent are her witcheries! Well I know her; so dost thou and those her victims too.

HEL. Menelaus! this prelude well may fill me with alarm; for I am haled with violence by thy servants' hands and brought before these tents. Still, though I am well-nigh sure thou hatest me, yet would I fain inquire what thou and Hellas have decided about my life.

MEN. To judge thy case required no great exactness; the host with one consent,—that host whom thou didst wrong,—handed thee over to me to die.

HEL. May I answer this decision, proving that my death, if to die I am, will be unjust?

MEN. I came not to argue, but to slay thee.

HEC. Hear her, Menelaus; let her not die for want of that, and let me answer her again, for thou knowest naught of her villainies in Troy; and the whole case, if thus summed up, will insure her death against all chance of an escape.

MEN. This boon needs leisure; still, if she wishes to speak, the leave is given. Yet will I grant her this because of thy words, that she may hear them, and not for her own sake.

HEL. Perhaps thou wilt not answer me, from counting me a foe, whether my words seem good or ill. Yet will I put my charges and thine over against each other, and then reply to the accusations I suppose thou wilt advance against me. First, then, she was the author of these troubles by giving birth to Paris; next, old Priam ruined Troy and me, because he did not slay his babe Alexander, baleful semblance of a fire-brand, long ago. Hear what followed. This Paris was to judge the claims of three rival goddesses; so Pallas offered him command of all the Phrygians, and the destruction of Hellas; Hera promised he should spread his dominion over Asia, and the utmost bounds of Europe, if he would decide for her; but Cypris spoke in rapture of my loveliness, and promised him this boon, if she should have the preference o'er those twain for beauty; now mark the inference I deduce from this; Cypris won the day o'er them, and thus far hath my marriage proved of benefit to Hellas, that ye are not subject to barbarian rule, neither vanquished in the strife, nor yet by tyrants crushed. What Hellas gained, was ruin to me, a victim for my beauty sold, and now am I reproached for that which should have set a crown upon my head. But thou wilt say I am silent on the real matter at issue, how it was I started forth and left thy house by stealth. With no mean goddess at his side he came, my evil genius, call him Alexander or Paris, as thou wilt; and him didst thou, thrice guilty wretch, leave behind thee in thy house, and sail away from Sparta to the land of Crete. Enough of this! For all that followed I must question my own heart, not thee; what frantic thought led me to follow the stranger from thy house, traitress to my country and my home? Punish the goddess, show thyself more mighty e'en than Zeus, who, though he lords it o'er the other gods, is yet her slave; wherefore I may well be pardoned. Still, from hence thou mightest draw a specious argument against me; when Paris died, and Earth concealed his corpse, I should have left his house and sought the Argive fleet, since my marriage was no longer in the hands of gods. That was what I fain had done; yea, and the warders on the towers and watchmen on the walls can bear me witness, for oft they found me seeking to let myself down stealthily by cords from the battlements; but there was that new husband, Deiphobus, that carried me off by force to be his wife against the will of Troy. How then, my lord, could I be justly put to death by thee, with any show of right, seeing that he wedded me against my will, and those my other natural gifts have served a bitter slavery, instead of leading on to triumph? If 'tis thy will indeed to master gods, that very wish displays thy folly.

CHO.   O my royal mistress, defend thy children's and thy country's cause, bringing to naught her persuasive arguments, for she pleads well in spite of all her villainy; 'tis monstrous this!

HEC.   First will I take up the cause of those goddesses, and prove how she perverts the truth. For I can ne'er believe that Hera or the maiden Pallas would have been guilty of such folly, as to sell, the one, her Argos to barbarians, or that Pallas e'er would make her Athens subject to the Phrygians, coming as they did in mere wanton sport to Ida to contest the palm of beauty. For why should goddess Hera set her heart so much on such a prize? Was it to win a nobler lord than Zeus? or was Athena bent on finding 'mongst the gods a husband, she who in her dislike of marriage won from her sire the boon of remaining unwed? Seek not to impute folly to the goddesses, in the attempt to gloze o'er thy own sin; never wilt thou persuade the wise. Next thou hast said, — what well may make men jeer, — that Cypris came with my son to the house of Menelaus. Could she not have stayed quietly in heaven and brought thee and Amyclæ to boot to Ilium? Nay! my son was passing fair, and when thou sawest him thy fancy straight became thy Cypris; for every sensual act that men commit, they lay upon this goddess, and rightly does her name of Aphrodite begin the word for "senselessness"; so when thou didst catch sight of him in gorgeous foreign garb, ablaze with gold, thy senses utterly forsook thee. Yea, for in Argos thou hadst moved in simple state, but, once free of Sparta, 'twas thy fond hope to deluge by thy lavish outlay Phrygia's town, that flowed with gold; nor was the palace of Menelaus rich enough for thy luxury to riot in. Ha! my son carried thee off by force, so thou sayest; what Spartan saw this? what cry for help didst thou ever raise, though Castor was still alive, a vigorous youth, and his brother also, not yet amid the stars? Then when thou wert come to Troy, and the Argives were on thy track, and the mortal combat was begun, whenever tidings came to thee of Menelaus' prowess, him wouldst thou praise, to grieve my son, because he had so powerful a rival in his love; but if so the Trojans prospered, Menelaus was nothing to thee. Thy eye was fixed on Fortune, and by such practice wert thou careful to follow in her steps, careless of virtue's cause. And then, in spite of all, thou dost assert that thou didst try to let thyself down from the towers by stealth with twisted cords, as if loth to stay? Pray then, wert thou ever found fastening the noose about thy neck, or whetting the knife, as a noble wife would have done in regret for her former husband? And yet full oft I advised thee saying, "Get thee gone, daughter, and let my sons take other brides; I will help thee to steal away, and convey thee to the Achæan fleet; oh end the strife 'twixt us and Hellas!" But this was bitter in thy ears. For thou wert wantoning in Alexander's house, fain to have obeisance done thee by barbarians. Yes, 'twas a proud time for thee; and now after all this thou hast bedizened thyself, and come forth and hast dared to appear under the same sky as thy husband, revolting wretch! Better hadst thou come in tattered raiment, cowering humbly in terror, with hair shorn short, if for thy past sins thy feeling were one of shame rather than effrontery. O Menelaus, hear the conclusion of my argument; crown Hellas by slaying her as she deserves, and establish this law for all others of her sex, e'en death to every traitress to her husband.

CHO. Avenge thee, Menelaus, on thy wife, as is worthy of thy home and ancestors, clear thyself from the reproach of effeminacy at the lips of Hellas, and let thy foes see thy spirit.

MEN. Thy thoughts with mine do coincide, that she, without constraint, left my palace, and sought a stranger's love, and now Cypris is introduced for mere bluster. Away to those who shall stone thee, and by thy speedy death requite the weary toils of the Achæans, that thou mayst learn not to bring shame on me!

HEL. Oh, by thy knees, I implore thee, impute not that heaven-sent affliction to me, nor slay me; pardon, I entreat!

HEC. Be not false to thy allies, whose death this woman caused; on their behalf, and for my children's sake, I sue to thee.

MEN. Peace, reverend dame; to her I pay no heed. Lo! I bid my servants take her hence, aboard the ship, wherein she is to sail.

HEC. Oh never let her set foot within the same ship as thee.

MEN. How now? is she heavier than of yore?

HEC. Who loveth once, must love alway.

MEN. Why, that depends how those we love are minded. But thy wish shall be granted; she shall not set foot upon the same ship with me; for thy advice is surely sound; and when she comes to Argos she shall die a shameful death as is her due, and impress the need of chastity on all her sex; no easy task; yet shall her fate strike their foolish hearts with terror, e'en though they be more lost to shame than she.

[_Exit_ MENELAUS, _dragging_ HELEN _with him._]

CHO. So then thou hast delivered into Achæa's hand, O Zeus, thy shrine in Ilium and thy fragrant altar, the offerings of burnt sacrifice with smoke of myrrh to heaven uprising, and holy Pergamos, and glens of Ida tangled with the ivy's growth, where rills of melting snow pour down their flood, a holy sun-lit land that bounds the world and takes the god's first rays! Gone are thy sacrifices! gone the dancer's cheerful shout! gone the vigils of the gods as night closed in! Thy images of carven gold are now no more; and Phrygia's holy festivals, twelve times a year, at each full moon, are ended now. 'Tis this that filleth me with anxious thought whether thou, O king, seated on the sky, thy heavenly throne, carest at all that my city is destroyed, a prey to the furious fiery blast. Ah! my husband, fondly loved, thou art a wandering spectre; unwashed, unburied lies thy corpse, while o'er the sea the ship sped by wings will carry me to Argos, land of steeds, where stand Cyclopian walls of stone upreared to heaven. There in the gate the children gather, hanging round their mothers' necks, and weep their piteous lamentation, "O mother, woe is me! torn from thy sight Achæans bear me away from thee to their dark ship to row me o'er the deep to sacred Salamis or to the hill on the Isthmus, that o'er-looks two seas, the key to the gates of Pelops. Oh may the blazing thunderbolt, hurled in might from its holy home, smite the barque of Menelaus full amidships as it is crossing the Ægean main, since he is carrying me away in bitter sorrow from the shores of Ilium to be a slave in Hellas, while the daughter of Zeus still keeps her golden mirrors, delight of maidens' hearts. Never may he reach his home in Laconia or his father's hearth and home, nor come to the town of Pitane or the temple of the goddess with the gates of bronze, having taken as his captive her whose marriage brought disgrace on Hellas through its length and breadth and woful anguish on the streams of Simois! Ah me! ah me! new trou-bles on my country fall, to take the place of those that still are fresh! Behold, ye hapless wives of Troy, the corpse of Astyanax! whom the Danai have cruelly slain by hurling him from the bat-tlements.

[*Enter* TALTHYBIUS *and attendants,*
bearing the corpse of ASTYANAX *on* HECTOR's *shield.*]

TAL.   Hecuba, one ship alone delays its plashing oars, and it is soon to sail to the shores of Phthia freighted with the remnant of the spoils of Achilles' son; for Neoptolemus is already out at sea, having heard that new calamities have befallen Peleus, for Acastus, son of Pelias, hath banished him the realm. Wherefore he is gone, too quick to indulge in any delay, and with him goes Andromache, who drew many a tear from me what time she started hence, wail-ing her country and crying her farewell to Hector's tomb. And she craved her master leave to bury this poor dead child of Hector who breathed his last when from the turrets hurled, entreating too that he would not carry this shield, the terror of the Achæans—this shield with plates of brass wherewith his father would gird him-self—to the home of Peleus or to the same bridal bower whither she, herself the mother of this corpse, would be led, a bitter sight to her, but let her bury the child therein instead of in a coffin of cedar or a tomb of stone, and to thy hands commit the corpse that thou mayst deck it with robes and garlands as best thou canst with thy present means; for she is far away and her master's haste pre-vented her from burying the child herself. So we, when thou the corpse hast decked, will heap the earth above and set thereon a spear; but do thou with thy best speed perform thy allotted task; one toil however have I already spared thee, for I crossed Scamander's stream and bathed the corpse and cleansed its wounds. But now will I go to dig a grave for him, that our united efforts shortening our task may speed our ship towards home.

[*Exit* TALTHYBIUS.

HEC. Place the shield upon the ground, Hector's shield so deftly rounded, a piteous sight, a bitter grief for me to see. O ye Achæans, more reason have ye to boast of your prowess than your wisdom! Why have ye in terror of this child been guilty of a murder never matched before? Did ye fear that some day he would rear again the fallen walls of Troy? It seems then ye were nothing after all, when, though Hector's fortunes in the war were prosperous and he had ten thousand other arms to back him, we still were daily overmatched; and yet, now that our city is taken and every Phrygian slain, ye fear a tender babe like this! Out upon his fear! say I, who fears, but never yet hath reasoned out the cause. Ah! my beloved, thine is a piteous death indeed! Hadst thou died for thy city, when thou hadst tasted of the sweets of manhood, of marriage, and of god-like power o'er others, then wert thou blest, if aught herein is blest. But now after one glimpse, one dream thereof thou knowest them no more, my child, and hast no joy of them, though heir to all. Ah, poor babe! how sadly have thy own father's walls, those towers that Loxias reared, shorn from thy head the locks thy mother fondled, and so oft caressed, from which through fractured bones the face of murder grins, — briefly to dismiss my shocking theme. O hands, how sweet the likeness ye retain of his father, and yet ye lie limp in your sockets before me! Dear mouth, so often full of words of pride, death hath closed thee, and thou hast not kept the promise thou didst make, when nestling in my robe, "Ah, mother mine, many a lock of my hair will I cut off for thee, and to thy tomb will lead my troops of friends, taking a fond farewell of thee." But now 'tis not thy hand that buries me, but I, on whom is come old age with loss of home and children, am burying thee, a tender child untimely slain. Ah me! those kisses numberless, the nurture that I gave to thee, those sleepless nights—they all are lost! What shall the bard inscribe upon thy tomb about thee? "Argives once for fear of him slew this child!" Foul shame should that inscription be to Hellas. O child, though thou hast no part in all thy father's wealth, yet shalt thou have his brazen shield wherein to find a tomb. Ah! shield that didst keep safe the comely arm of Hector, now hast thou lost thy valiant keeper! How fair upon thy handle lies his imprint, and on the rim, that circles round the targe, are marks of sweat, that trickled oft from Hector's brow as he pressed it 'gainst his beard in battle's stress. Come, bring forth, from such store as we have, adornment for the hapless dead, for fortune gives no chance now for offerings fair; yet of such as I possess, shalt thou receive these gifts. Foolish mortal he! who thinks his luck secure and so rejoices; for fortune, like a madman in her moods, springs towards this man, then towards that; and none ever experiences the same unchanging luck.

CHO.   Lo! all is ready and they are bringing at thy bidding from the spoils of Troy garniture to put upon the dead.

HEC.   Ah! my child, 'tis not as victor o'er thy comrades with horse or bow,—customs Troy esteems, without pursuing them to excess,—that Hector's mother decks thee now with ornaments from the store that once was thine, though now hath Helen, whom the gods abhor, reft thee of thine own, yea, and robbed thee of thy life and caused thy house to perish root and branch.

CHO.   Woe! thrice woe! my heart is touched, and thou the cause, my mighty prince in days now passed!

HEC.   About thy body now I swathe this Phrygian robe of honour, which should have clad thee on thy marriage-day, wedded to the noblest of Asia's daughters. Thou too, dear shield of Hector, victorious parent of countless triumphs past, accept thy crown, for though thou share the dead child's tomb, death cannot touch thee; for thou dost merit honours far beyond those arms that the crafty knave Odysseus won.

CHO.   Alas! ah me! thee, O child, shall earth take to her breast, a cause for bitter weeping. Mourn, thou mother!

HEC.   Ah me!

CHO.   Wail for the dead.

HEC.   Woe is me!

CHO.   Alas! for thy unending sorrow!

HEC.   Thy wounds in part will I bind up with bandages, a wretched leech in name alone, without reality; but for the rest, thy sire must look to that amongst the dead.

CHO.   Smite, oh smite upon thy head with frequent blow of hand. Woe is me!

HEC.   My kind, good friends!

CHO.   Speak out, Hecuba, the word that was on thy lips.

HEC.   It seems the only things that heaven concerns itself about are my troubles and Troy hateful in their eyes above all other cities. In vain did we sacrifice to them. Had not the god caught us in his grip and plunged us headlong 'neath the earth, we should have been unheard of, nor ever sung in Muses' songs, furnishing to bards of after-days a subject for their minstrelsy. Go, bury now in his poor tomb the dead, wreathed all duly as befits a corpse. And yet I deem it makes but little difference to the dead, although they get a gorgeous funeral; for this is but a cause of idle pride to the living. [*The corpse is carried off to burial.*

CHO. Alas! for thy unhappy mother, who o'er thy corpse hath closed the high hopes of her life! Born of a noble stock, counted most happy in thy lot, ah! what a tragic death is thine! Ha! who are those I see on yonder pinnacles darting to and fro with flaming torches in their hands? Some new calamity will soon on Troy alight.

[*Soldiers are seen on the battlements of Troy, torch in hand.*]

TAL. Ye captains, whose allotted task it is to fire this town of Priam, to you I speak. No longer keep the firebrand idle in your hands, but launch the flame, that when we have destroyed the city of Ilium we may set forth in gladness on our homeward voyage from Troy. And you, ye sons of Troy,—to let my orders take at once a double form—start for the Achæan ships for your departure hence, soon as ever the leaders of the host blow loud and clear upon the trumpet. And thou, unhappy grey-haired dame, follow; for yonder come servants from Odysseus to fetch thee, for to him thou art assigned by lot to be a slave far from thy country.

HEC. Ah, woe is me! This surely is the last, the utmost limit this, of all my sorrows; forth from my land I go; my city is ablaze with flame. Yet, thou aged foot, make one painful struggle to hasten, that I may say a farewell to this wretched town. O Troy, that erst hadst such a grand career amongst barbarian towns, soon wilt thou be reft of that splendid name. Lo! they are burning thee, and leading us e'en now from our land to slavery. Great gods! Yet why call on the gods? They did not hearken e'en aforetime to our call. Come, let us rush into the flames, for to die with my country in its blazing ruin were a noble death for me.

TAL. Thy sorrows drive thee frantic, poor lady. Go, lead her hence, make no delay, for ye must deliver her into the hand of Odysseus, conveying to him his prize.

HEC. O son of Cronos, prince of Phrygia, father of our race, dost thou behold our sufferings now, unworthy of the stock of Dardanus?

CHO. He sees them, but our mighty city is a city no more, and Troy's day is done.

HEC.   Woe! thrice woe upon me! Ilium is ablaze; the homes of Pergamos and its towering walls are now one sheet of flame.

CHO.   As the smoke soars on wings to heaven, so sinks our city to the ground before the spear. With furious haste both fire and foeman's spear devour each house.

HEC.   Hearken, my children, hear your mother's voice.

CHO.   Thou art calling on the dead with voice of lamentation.

HEC.   Yea, as I stretch my aged limbs upon the ground, and beat upon the earth with both my hands.

CHO.   I follow thee and kneel, invoking from the nether world my hapless husband.

HEC.   I am being dragged and hurried away—

CHO.   O the sorrow of that cry!

HEC.   From my own dear country, to dwell beneath a master's roof. Woe is me! O Priam, Priam, slain, unburied, left without a friend, naught dost thou know of my cruel fate.

CHO.   No, for o'er his eyes black death hath drawn his pall,—a holy man by sinners slain!

HEC.   Woe for the temples of the gods! Woe for our dear city!

CHO.   Woe!

HEC.   Murderous flame and foeman's spear are now your lot.

CHO.   Soon will ye tumble to your own loved soil, and be forgotten.

HEC.   And the dust, mounting to heaven on wings like smoke, will rob me of the sight of my home.

CHO.   The name of my country will pass into obscurity; all is scattered far and wide, and hapless Troy has ceased to be.

HEC.   Did ye hear that and know its purport?

CHO.   Aye, 'twas the crash of the citadel.

HEC.   The shock will whelm our city utterly. O woe is me! trembling, quaking limbs, support my footsteps! away! to face the day that begins thy slavery.

CHO.   Woe for our unhappy town! And yet to the Achæan fleet advance.

HEC.   Woe for thee, O land that nursed my little babes!

CHO.   Ah! woe!

HIPPOLYTUS

DRAMATIS PERSONÆ

APHRODITE.

HIPPOLYTUS.

ATTENDANTS OF HIPPOLYTUS.

CHORUS OF TRŒZENIAN WOMEN.

NURSE OF PHÆDRA.

PHÆDRA.

THESEUS.

FIRST MESSENGER.

SECOND MESSENGER.

ARTEMIS.

SCENE.—Before the palace of Pittheus at Trœzen.

HIPPOLYTUS

APH. Wide o'er man my realm extends, and proud the name that I, the goddess Cypris, bear, both in heaven's courts and 'mongst all those who dwell within the limits of the sea and the bounds of Atlas, beholding the sun-god's light; those that respect my power I advance to honour, but bring to ruin all who vaunt themselves at me. For even in the race of gods this feeling finds a home, even pleasure at the honour men pay them. And the truth of this I soon will show; for that son of Theseus, born of the Amazon, Hippolytus, whom holy Pittheus taught, alone of all the dwellers in this land of Trœzen, calls me vilest of the deities. Love he scorns, and, as for marriage, will none of it; but Artemis, daughter of Zeus, sister of Phœbus, he doth honour, counting her the chief of goddesses, and ever through the greenwood, attendant on his virgin goddess, he clears the earth of wild beasts with his fleet hounds, enjoying the comradeship of one too high for mortal ken. 'Tis not this I grudge him, no! why should I? But for his sins against me, I will this very day take vengeance on Hippolytus; for long ago I cleared the ground of many obstacles, so it needs but trifling toil. For as he came one day from the home of Pittheus to witness the solemn mystic rites and be initiated therein in Pandion's land, Phædra, his father's noble wife, caught sight of him, and by my designs she found her heart was seized with wild desire. And ere she came to this Trœzenian realm, a temple did she rear to Cypris hard by the rock of Pallas where it o'erlooks this country, for love of the youth in another land; and to win his love in days to come she called after his name the temple she had founded for the goddess. Now, when Theseus left the land of Cecrops, flying the pollution of the blood of Pallas' sons, and with his wife sailed to this shore, content to suffer exile for a year, then began the wretched wife to pine away in silence, moaning 'neath love's cruel scourge, and none of her servants knows what ails her. But this passion of hers must not fail thus. No, I will discover the

31

matter to Theseus, and all shall be laid bare. Then will the father slay his child, my bitter foe, by curses, for the lord Poseidon granted this boon to Theseus; three wishes of the god to ask, nor ever ask in vain. So Phædra is to die, an honoured death 'tis true, but still to die; for I will not let her suffering outweigh the payment of such forfeit by my foes as shall satisfy my honour. But lo! I see the son of Theseus coming hither—Hippolytus, fresh from the labours of the chase. I will get me hence. At his back follows a long train of retainers, in joyous cries of revelry uniting and hymns of praise to Artemis, his goddess; for little he recks that Death hath oped his gates for him, and that this is his last look upon the light.

HIP.   Come follow, friends, singing to Artemis, daughter of Zeus, throned in the sky, whose votaries we are.

ATT.   Lady goddess, awful queen, daughter of Zeus, all hail! hail! child of Latona and of Zeus, peerless mid the virgin choir, who hast thy dwelling in heaven's wide mansions at thy noble father's court, in the golden house of Zeus.

HIP.   All hail! most beauteous Artemis, lovelier far than all the daughters of Olympus! For thee, O mistress mine, I bring this woven wreath, culled from a virgin meadow, where nor shepherd dares to herd his flock nor ever scythe hath mown, but o'er the mead unshorn the bee doth wing its way in spring; and with the dew from rivers drawn purity that garden tends. Such as know no cunning lore, yet in whose nature self-control, made perfect, hath a home, these may pluck the flowers, but not the wicked world. Accept, I pray, dear mistress, mine this chaplet from my holy hand to crown thy locks of gold; for I, and none other of mortals, have this high guerdon, to be with thee, with thee converse, hearing thy voice, though not thy face beholding. So be it mine to end my life as I began.

ATT.   My prince! we needs must call upon the gods, our lords, so wilt thou listen to a friendly word from me?

HIP.   Why, that will I! else were I proved a fool.

ATT.   Dost know, then, the way of the world?

HIP.   Not I; but wherefore such a question?

ATT.   It hates reserve which careth not for all men's love.

HIP.   And rightly too; reserve in man is ever galling.

ATT.   But there's a charm in courteous affability?

HIP.   The greatest surely; aye, and profit, too, at trifling cost.

ATT.   Dost think the same law holds in heaven as well?

HIP.   I trow it doth, since all our laws we men from heaven draw.

ATT.   Why, then, dost thou neglect to greet an august goddess?

HIP.   Whom speak'st thou of? Keep watch upon thy tongue lest it some mischief cause.

ATT.   Cypris I mean, whose image is stationed o'er thy gate.

HIP.   I greet her from afar, preserving still my chastity.

ATT.   Yet is she an august goddess, far renowned on earth.

HIP.   'Mongst gods as well as men we have our several preferences.

ATT.   I wish thee luck, and wisdom too, so far as thou dost need it.

HIP.   No god, whose worship craves the night, hath charms for me.

ATT.   My son, we should avail us of the gifts that gods confer.

HIP.   Go in, my faithful followers, and make ready food within the house; a well-filled board hath charms after the chase is o'er. Rub down my steeds ye must, that when I have had my fill I may yoke them to the chariot and give them proper exercise. As for thy Queen of Love, a long farewell to her.   [*Exit* HIPPOLYTUS.

ATT.   Meantime I with sober mind, for I must not copy my young master, do offer up my prayer to thy image, lady Cypris, in such words as it becomes a slave to use. But thou should'st pardon all, who, in youth's impetuous heat, speak idle words of thee; make as though thou hearest not, for gods must needs be wiser than the sons of men.

CHO.   A rock there is, where, as they say, the ocean dew distils, and from its beetling brow it pours a copious stream for pitchers to be dipped therein; 'twas here I had a friend washing robes of purple in the trickling stream, and she was spreading them out on the face of a warm sunny rock; from her I had the tidings, first of all, that my mistress was wasting on the bed of sickness, pent within her house, a thin veil o'ershadowing her head of golden hair. And this is the third day I hear that she hath closed her lovely lips and denied her chaste body all sustenance, eager to hide her suffering and reach death's cheerless bourn. Maiden, thou must be possessed, by Pan made frantic or by Hecate, or by the Corybantes dread, and Cybele the mountain mother. Or maybe thou hast sinned against Dictynna, huntress-queen, and art wasting for thy guilt in sacrifice unoffered. For she doth range o'er lakes' expanse and past the bounds of earth upon the ocean's tossing billows. Or doth some rival in thy house beguile thy lord, the captain of Erechtheus' sons, that hero nobly born, to secret amours hid from thee? Or hath some mariner sailing hither from Crete reached this port that sailors love, with evil tidings for our queen, and she with sorrow for her grievous fate is to her bed confined? Yea, and oft o'er woman's wayward nature settles a feeling of miserable perplexity, arising from labour-pains or passionate desire. I, too, have felt at times this sharp thrill shoot through me, but I would cry to

Artemis, queen of archery, who comes from heaven to aid us in our travail, and thanks to heaven's grace she ever comes at my call with welcome help. Look! where the aged nurse is bringing her forth from the house before the door, while on her brow the cloud of gloom is deepening. My soul longs to learn what is her grief, the canker that is wasting our queen's fading charms.

NUR.   O, the ills of mortal men! the cruel diseases they endure! What can I do for thee? from what refrain? Here is the bright sun-light, here the azure sky; lo! we have brought thee on thy bed of sickness without the palace; for all thy talk was of coming hither, but soon back to thy chamber wilt thou hurry. Disappointment follows fast with thee, thou hast no joy in aught for long; the present has no power to please; on something absent next thy heart is set. Better be sick than tend the sick; the first is but a single ill, the last unites mental grief with manual toil. Man's whole life is full of anguish; no respite from his woes he finds; but if there is aught to love beyond this life, night's dark pall doth wrap it round. And so we show our mad love of this life because its light is shed on earth, and because we know no other, and have naught revealed to us of all our earth may hide; and trusting to fables we drift at random.

PHÆ.   Lift my body, raise my head! My limbs are all unstrung, kind friends. O handmaids, lift my arms, my shapely arms. The tire on my head is too heavy for me to wear; away with it, and let my tresses o'er my shoulders fall.

NUR.   Be of good heart, dear child; toss not so wildly to and fro. Lie still, be brave, so wilt thou find thy sickness easier to bear; suffering for mortals is nature's iron law.

PHÆ.   Ah! would I could draw a draught of water pure from some dew-fed spring, and lay me down to rest in the grassy meadow 'neath the poplar's shade!

NUR.   My child, what wild speech is this? O say not such things in public, wild whirling words of frenzy bred!

PHÆ.   Away to the mountain take me! to the wood, to the pine-trees I will go, where hounds pursue the prey, hard on the scent of dappled fawns. Ye gods! what joy to hark them on, to grasp the barbed dart, to poise Thessalian hunting-spears close to my golden hair, then let them fly.

NUR.   Why, why, my child, these anxious cares? What hast thou to do with the chase? Why so eager for the flowing spring, when hard by these towers stands a hill well watered, whence thou may'st freely draw?

PHÆ.   O Artemis, who watchest o'er sea-beat Limna and the racecourse thundering to the horse's hoofs, would I were upon thy plains curbing Venetian steeds!

NUR. Why betray thy frenzy in these wild whirling words? Now thou wert for hasting hence to the hills away to hunt wild beasts, and now thy yearning is to drive the steed over the waveless sands. This needs a cunning seer to say what god it is that reins thee from the course, distracting thy senses, child.

PHÆ. Ah me! alas! what have I done? Whither have I strayed, my senses leaving? Mad, mad! stricken by some demon's curse! Woe is me! Cover my head again, nurse. Shame fills me for the words I have spoken. Hide me then; from my eyes the tear-drops stream, and for very shame I turn them away. 'Tis painful coming to one's senses again, and madness, evil though it be, has this advantage, that one has no knowledge of reason's overthrow.

NUR. There then I cover thee; but when will death hide my body in the grave? Many a lesson length of days is teaching me. Yea, mortal men should pledge themselves to moderate friendships only, not to such as reach the very heart's core; affection's ties should be light upon them to let them slip or draw them tight. For one poor heart to grieve for twain, as I do for my mistress, is a burden sore to bear. Men say that too engrossing pursuits in life more oft cause disappointment than pleasure, and too oft are foes to health. Wherefore I do not praise excess so much as moderation, and with me wise men will agree.

CHO. O aged dame, faithful nurse of Phædra, our queen, we see her sorry plight; but what it is that ails her we cannot discern, so fain would learn of thee and hear thy opinion.

NUR. I question her, but am no wiser, for she will not answer.

CHO. Nor tell what source these sorrows have?

NUR. The same answer thou must take, for she is dumb on every point.

CHO. How weak and wasted is her body!

NUR. What marvel? 'tis three days now since she has tasted food.

CHO. Is this infatuation, or an attempt to die?

NUR. 'Tis death she courts; such fasting aims at ending life.

CHO. A strange story! is her husband satisfied?

NUR. She hides from him her sorrow, and vows she is not ill.

CHO. Can he not guess it from her face?

NUR. He is not now in his own country.

CHO. But dost not thou insist in thy endeavour to find out her complaint, her crazy mind?

NUR. I have tried every plan, and all in vain; yet not even now will I relax my zeal, that thou too, if thou stayest, mayst witness my devotion to my unhappy mistress. Come, come, my darling child, let us forget, the twain of us, our former words; be thou more mild, smoothing that sullen brow and changing the current of thy thought, and I, if in aught before I failed in humouring thee, will let that be and find some better course. If thou art sick with ills thou canst not name, there be women here to help to set thee right; but if thy trouble can to men's ears be divulged, speak, that physicians may pronounce on it. Come, then, why so dumb? Thou shouldst not so remain, my child, but scold me if I speak amiss, or, if I give good counsel, yield assent. One word, one look this way! Ah me! Friends, we waste our toil to no purpose; we are as far away as ever; she would not relent to my arguments then, nor is she yielding now. Well, grow more stubborn than the sea, yet be assured of this, that if thou diest thou art a traitress to thy children, for they will ne'er inherit their father's halls, nay, by that knightly queen the Amazon who bore a son to lord it over thine, a bastard born but not a bastard bred, whom well thou knowest, e'en Hippolytus.

PHÆ. Oh! oh!

NUR. Ha! doth that touch the quick?

PHÆ. Thou hast undone me, nurse; I do adjure by the gods, mention that man no more.

NUR. There now! thou art thyself again, but e'en yet refusest to aid thy children and preserve thy life.

PHÆ. My babes I love, but there is another storm that buffets me.

NUR. Daughter, are thy hands from bloodshed pure?

PHÆ. My hands are pure, but on my soul there rests a stain.

NUR. The issue of some enemy's secret witchery?

PHÆ. A friend is my destroyer, one unwilling as myself.

NUR. Hath Theseus wronged thee in any wise?

PHÆ. Never may I prove untrue to him!

NUR. Then what strange mystery is there that drives thee on to die?

PHÆ. O, let my sin and me alone! 'tis not 'gainst thee I sin.

NUR. Never willingly! and, if I fail, 'twill rest at thy door.

PHÆ. How now? thou usest force in clinging to my hand.

NUR. Yea, and I will never loose my hold upon thy knees.

PHÆ. Alas for thee! my sorrows, shouldst thou learn them, would recoil on thee.

NUR. What keener grief for me than failing to win thee?

PHÆ. 'Twill be death to thee; though to me that brings renown.

NUR. And dost thou then conceal this boon despite my prayers?

PHÆ. I do, for 'tis out of shame I am planning an honourable escape.

NUR. Tell it, and thine honour shall the brighter shine.

PHÆ. Away, I do conjure thee; loose my hand.

NUR. I will not, for the boon thou shouldst have granted me is denied.

PHÆ. I will grant it out of reverence for thy holy suppliant touch.

NUR. Henceforth I hold my peace; 'tis thine to speak from now.

PHÆ. Ah! hapless mother, what a love was thine!

NUR. Her love for the bull? daughter, or what meanest thou?

PHÆ. And woe to thee! my sister, bride of Dionysus.

NUR. What ails thee, child? speaking ill of kith and kin.

PHÆ. Myself the third to suffer! how am I undone!

NUR. Thou strik'st me dumb! Where will this history end?

PHÆ. That "love" has been our curse from time long past.

NUR. I know no more of what I fain would learn.

PHÆ. Ah! would thou couldst say for me what I have to tell.

NUR. I am no prophetess to unriddle secrets.

PHÆ. What is it they mean when they talk of people being in "love?"

NUR. At once the sweetest and the bitterest thing, my child.

PHÆ. I shall only find the latter half.

NUR. Ha! my child, art thou in love?

PHÆ. The Amazon's son, whoever he may be, —

NUR. Mean'st thou Hippolytus?

PHÆ. 'Twas thou, not I, that spoke his name.

NUR. O heavens! what is this, my child? Thou hast ruined me. Outrageous! friends; I will not live and bear it; hateful is life, hateful to mine eyes the light. This body I resign, will cast it off, and rid me of existence by my death. Farewell, my life is o'er. Yea, for the chaste have wicked passions, 'gainst their will maybe, but still they have. Cypris, it seems, is not a goddess after all, but something greater far, for she hath been the ruin of my lady and of me and our whole family.

CHO. O, too clearly didst thou hear our queen uplift her voice to tell her startling tale of piteous suffering. Come death ere I reach thy state of feeling, loved mistress. O horrible! woe, for these miseries! woe, for the sorrows on which mortals feed! Thou art undone! thou hast disclosed thy sin to heaven's light. What hath each passing day and every hour in store for thee? Some strange event will come to pass in this house. For it is no longer uncertain where the star of thy love is setting, thou hapless daughter of Crete.

PHÆ. Ladies of Trœzen, who dwell here upon the frontier edge of Pelops' land, oft ere now in heedless mood through the long hours of night have I wondered why man's life is spoiled; and it seems to me their evil case is not due to any natural fault of judgment, for there be many dowered with sense, but we must view the matter in this light; by teaching and experience we learn the right but neglect it in practice, some from sloth, others from preferring pleasure of some kind or other to duty. Now life has many pleasures, protracted talk, and leisure, that seductive evil; likewise there is shame which is of two kinds, one a noble quality, the other a curse to families; but if for each its proper time were clearly known, these twain could not have had the selfsame letters to denote them. So then since I had made up my mind on these points, 'twas not likely any drug would alter it and make me think the contrary. And I will tell thee too the way my judgment went. When love wounded me, I bethought me how I best might bear the smart. So from that day forth I began to hide in silence what I suffered. For I put no faith in counsellors, who know well to lecture others for presumption, yet themselves have countless troubles of their own. Next I did devise noble endurance of these wanton thoughts, striving by continence for victory. And last when I could not succeed in mastering love hereby, methought it best to die; and none can gainsay my purpose. For fain I would my virtue should to all appear, my shame have few to witness it. I knew my sickly passion now; to yield to it I saw how infamous; and more, I learnt to know so well that I was but a woman, a thing the world detests. Curses, hideous curses on that wife, who first did shame her marriage-vow for lovers other than her lord! 'Twas from noble families this curse began to spread among our sex. For when the noble countenance disgrace, poor folk of course will think that it is right. Those too I hate who make profession of purity, though in secret reckless sinners. How can these, queen Cypris, ocean's child, e'er look their husbands in the face? do they never feel one guilty thrill that their accomplice, night, or the chambers of their house will find a voice and speak? This it is that calls on me to die, kind friends, that so I may ne'er be found to have disgraced my lord, or the children I have born; no! may they grow up and dwell in glorious Athens, free to speak and act, heirs to such fair fame as a mother can bequeath. For to know that father or mother have sinned doth turn the stoutest heart to slavishness. This alone, men say, can stand the buffets of life's battle, a just and virtuous soul in whomsoever found. For time unmasks the villain sooner or later, holding up to them a mirror as to some blooming maid. 'Mongst such may I be never seen!

CHO.   Now look! how fair is chastity however viewed, whose fruit is good repute amongst men.

NUR.   My queen, 'tis true thy tale of woe, but lately told, did for the moment strike me with wild alarm, but now I do reflect upon my

foolishness; second thoughts are often best even with men. Thy
fate is no uncommon one nor past one's calculations; thou art
stricken by the passion Cypris sends. Thou art in love; what won-
der? so are many more. Wilt thou, because thou lov'st, destroy thyself? 'Tis little gain, I trow, for those who love or yet may love their
fellows, if death must be their end; for though the Love-Queen's
onset in her might is more than man can bear, yet doth she gen-
tly visit yielding hearts, and only when she finds a proud unnatural
spirit, doth she take and mock it past belief. Her path is in the sky,
and mid the ocean's surge she rides; from her all nature springs;
she sows the seeds of love, inspires the warm desire to which we
sons of earth all owe our being. They who have aught to do with
books of ancient scribes, or themselves engage in studious pursuits, know how Zeus of Semele was enamoured, how the bright-
eyed goddess of the Dawn once stole Cephalus to dwell in heaven
for the love she bore him; yet these in heaven abide nor shun the
gods' approach, content, I trow, to yield to their misfortune. Wilt
thou refuse to yield? thy sire, it seems, should have begotten thee
on special terms or with different gods for masters, if in these laws
thou wilt not acquiesce. How many, prithee, men of sterling
sense, when they see their wives unfaithful, make as though they
saw it not? How many fathers, when their sons have gone astray,
assist them in their amours? 'tis part of human wisdom to conceal
the deed of shame. Nor should man aim at excessive refinement
in his life; for they cannot with exactness finish e'en the roof that
covers in a house; and how dost thou, after falling into so deep a
pit, think to escape? Nay, if thou hast more of good than bad, thou
wilt fare exceeding well, thy human nature considered. O cease,
my darling child, from evil thoughts, let wanton pride be gone, for
this is naught else, this wish to rival gods in perfectness. Face thy
love; 'tis heaven's will thou shouldst. Sick thou art, yet turn thy
sickness to some happy issue. For there are charms and spells to
soothe the soul; surely some cure for thy disease will be found.
Men, no doubt, might seek it long and late if our women's minds
no scheme devise.

CHO.   Although she gives thee at thy present need the wiser counsel,
Phædra, yet do I praise thee. Still my praise may sound more
harsh and jar more cruelly on thy ear than her advice.

PHÆ.   'Tis even this, too plausible a tongue, that overthrows good governments and homes of men. We should not speak to please the
ear but point the path that leads to noble fame.

NUR.   What means this solemn speech? No need of rounded phrases;
but at once must we sound the prince, telling him frankly how it

is with thee. Had not thy life to such a crisis come, or wert thou with self-control endowed, ne'er would I to gratify thy passions have urged thee to this course; but now 'tis a struggle fierce to save thy life, and therefore less to blame.

PHÆ. Accursed proposal! peace, woman! never utter those shameful words again!

NUR. Shameful, maybe, yet for thee better than honour's code. Better this deed, if it shall save thy life, than that name thy pride will kill thee to retain.

PHÆ. I conjure thee, go no further! for thy words are plausible but infamous; for though as yet love has not undermined my soul, yet, if in specious words thou dress thy foul suggestion, I shall be beguiled into the snare from which I am now escaping.

NUR. If thou art of this mind, 'twere well thou ne'er hadst sinned; but as it is, hear me; for that is the next best course; I in my house have charms to soothe thy love,—'twas but now I thought of them;—these shall cure thee of thy sickness on no disgraceful terms, thy mind unhurt, if thou wilt be but brave. [But from him thou lovest we must get some token, a word or fragment of his robe, and thereby unite in one love's twofold stream.]

PHÆ. Is thy drug a salve or potion?

NUR. I cannot tell; be content, my child, to profit by it and ask no questions.

PHÆ. I fear me thou wilt prove too wise for me.

NUR. If thou fear this, confess thyself afraid of all; but why thy terror?

PHÆ. Lest thou shouldst breathe a word of this to Theseus' son.

NUR. Peace, my child! I will do all things well; only be thou, queen Cypris, ocean's child, my partner in the work! And for the rest of my purpose, it will be enough for me to tell it to our friends within the house.   [*Exit* NURSE.

CHO. O Love, Love, that from the eyes diffusest soft desire, bringing on the souls of those, whom thou dost camp against, sweet grace, O never in evil mood appear to me, nor out of time and tune approach! Nor fire nor meteor hurls a mightier bolt than Aphrodite's shaft shot by the hands of Love, the child of Zeus. Idly, idly by the streams of Alpheus and in the Pythian shrines of Phœbus, Hellas heaps the slaughtered steers; while Love we worship not, Love, the king of men, who holds the key to Aphrodite's sweetest bower,—worship not him who, when he comes, lays waste and marks his path to mortal hearts by wide-spread woe. There was that maiden in Œchalia, a girl unwed, that knew no wooer yet nor married joys; her did the queen of Love snatch from her home across the sea and gave unto Alcmena's son, mid blood and smoke and murderous marriage-hymns, to be to him a frantic fiend of hell; woe! woe for his wooing!

Ah! holy walls of Thebes, ah! fount of Dirce, ye could testify what course the love-queen follows. For with the blazing levin-bolt did she cut short the fatal marriage of Semele, mother of Zeus-born Bacchus. All things she doth inspire, dread goddess, winging her flight hither and thither like a bee.

PHÆ. Peace, ladies, peace! I am undone.

CHO. What, Phædra, is this dread event within thy house?

PHÆ. Hush! let me hear what those within are saying.

CHO. I am silent; this is surely the prelude to mischief.

PHÆ. Great gods! how awful are my sufferings!

CHO. What a cry was there! what loud alarm! say what sudden terror, lady, doth thy soul dismay.

PHÆ. I am undone. Stand here at the door and hear the noise arising in the house.

CHO. Thou art already by the bolted door; 'tis for thee to note the sounds that issue from within. And tell me, O tell me what mischief can be on foot.

PHÆ. 'Tis the son of the horse-loving Amazon who calls, Hippolytus, uttering foul curses on my servant.

CHO. I hear a noise, but cannot clearly tell which way it comes. Ah! 'tis through the door the sound reached thee.

PHÆ. Yes, yes, he is calling her plainly enough a go-between in vice, traitress to her master's honour.

CHO. Woe, woe is me! thou art betrayed, dear mistress! What counsel shall I give thee? thy secret is out; thou art utterly undone.

PHÆ. Ah me! ah me!

CHO. Betrayed by friends!

PHÆ. She hath ruined me by speaking of my misfortune; 'twas kindly meant, but an ill way to cure my malady.

CHO. O what wilt thou do now in thy cruel dilemma?

PHÆ. I only know one way, one cure for these my woes, and that is instant death.

HIP. O mother earth! O sun's unclouded orb! What words, unfit for any lips, have reached my ears!

NUR. Peace, my son, lest some one hear thy outcry.

HIP. I cannot hear such awful words and hold my peace.

NUR. I do implore thee by thy fair right hand.

HIP. Let go my hand, touch not my robe.

NUR. O by thy knees I pray, destroy me not utterly.

HIP. Why say this, if, as thou pretendest, thy lips are free from blame?

NUR. My son, this is no story to be noised abroad.

HIP.   A virtuous tale grows fairer told to many.

NUR.   Never dishonour thy oath, thy son.

HIP.   My tongue an oath did take, but not my heart.

NUR.   My son, what wilt thou do? destroy thy friends?

HIP.   Friends indeed! the wicked are no friends of mine.

NUR.   O pardon me; to err is only human, child.

HIP.   Great Zeus, why didst thou, to man's sorrow, put woman, evil counterfeit, to dwell where shines the sun? If thou wert minded that the human race should multiply, it was not from women they should have drawn their stock, but in thy temples they should have paid gold or iron or ponderous bronze and bought a family, each man proportioned to his offering, and so in independence dwelt, from women free. [But now as soon as ever we would bring this plague into our home we bring its fortune to the ground.] 'Tis clear from this how great a curse a woman is; the very father, that begot and nurtured her, to rid him of the mischief, gives her a dower and packs her off; while the husband, who takes the noxious weed into his home, fondly decks his sorry idol in fine raiment and tricks her out in robes, squandering by degrees, unhappy wight! his house's wealth. For he is in this dilemma; say his marriage has brought him good connections, he is glad then to keep the wife he loathes; or, if he gets a good wife but useless relations, he tries to stifle the bad luck with the good. But it is easiest for him who has settled in his house as wife a mere nobody, incapable from simplicity. I hate a clever woman; never may she set foot in *my* house who aims at knowing more than women need; for in these clever women Cypris implants a larger store of villainy, while the artless woman is by her shallow wit from levity debarred. No servant should ever have had access to a wife, but men should put to live with them beasts, which bite, not talk, in which case they could not speak to any one nor be answered back by them. But, as it is, the wicked in their chambers plot wickedness, and their servants carry it abroad. Even thus, vile wretch, thou cam'st to make me partner in an outrage on my father's honour; wherefore I must wash that stain away in running streams, dashing the water into my ears. How could I commit so foul a crime when by the very mention of it I feel myself polluted? Be well assured, woman, 'tis only my religious scruple saves thee. For had not I unawares been caught by an oath, 'fore heaven! I would not have refrained from telling all unto my father. But now I will from the house away, so long as Theseus is abroad, and will maintain strict silence. But, when my father comes, I will return and see how thou and thy mistress face him, and so shall I learn by

PHÆ. 'Tis well. But I, with all my thought, can but one way discover out of this calamity, that so I may secure my children's honour, and find myself some help as matters stand. For never, never will I bring shame upon my Cretan home, nor will I, to save one poor life, face Theseus after my disgrace.

CHO. Art thou bent then on some cureless woe?

PHÆ. On death; the means thereto must I devise myself.

CHO. Hush!

PHÆ. Do thou at least advise me well. For this very day shall I gladden Cypris, my destroyer, by yielding up my life, and shall own myself vanquished by cruel love. Yet shall my dying be another's curse, that he may learn not to exult at my misfortunes; but when he comes to share the self-same plague with me, he will take a lesson in wisdom.

CHO. O to be nestling 'neath some pathless cavern, there by god's creating hand to grow into a bird amid the wingèd tribes! Away would I soar to Adria's wave-beat shore and to the waters of Eridanus; where a father's hapless daughters in their grief for Phäethon distil into the glooming flood the amber brilliance of their tears. And to the apple-bearing strand of those minstrels in the west I then would come, where ocean's lord no more to sailors grants a passage o'er the deep dark main, finding there the heaven's holy bound, upheld by Atlas, where water from ambrosial founts wells up beside the couch of Zeus inside his halls, and holy earth, the bounteous mother, causes joy to spring in heavenly breasts. O white-winged bark, that o'er the booming ocean-wave didst bring my royal mistress from her happy home, to crown her queen 'mongst sorrow's brides! Surely evil omens from either port, at least from Crete, were with that ship, what time to glorious Athens it sped its way, and the crew made fast its twisted cable-ends upon the beach of Munychus, and on the land stept out. Whence comes it that her heart is crushed, cruelly afflicted by Aphrodite with unholy love; so she by bitter grief o'erwhelmed will tie a noose within her bridal bower to fit it to her fair white neck, too modest for this hateful lot in life, prizing o'er all her name and fame, and striving thus to rid her soul of passion's sting.

MES. Help! ho! To the rescue all who near the palace stand! She hath hung herself, our queen, the wife of Theseus.

CHO. Woe worth the day! the deed is done; our royal mistress is no more, dead she hangs in the dangling noose.

MES. Haste! some one bring a two-edged knife wherewith to cut the knot about her neck!

experience the extent of thy audacity. Perdition seize you both! [*To the audience.*] I can never satisfy my hate for women, no! not ever, though some say this is ever my theme, for of a truth they always are evil. So either let some one prove them chaste, or let me still trample on them for ever.

CHO. O the cruel, unhappy fate of women! What arts, what arguments have we, once we have made a slip, to loose by craft the tight-drawn knot?

PHÆ. I have met my deserts. O earth, O light of day! How can I escape the stroke of fate? How my pangs conceal, kind friends? What god will appear to help me, what mortal to take my part or help me in unrighteousness? The present calamity of my life admits of no escape. Most hapless I of all my sex!

CHO. Alas, alas! the deed is done, thy servant's schemes have gone awry, my queen, and all is lost.

PHÆ. Accursed woman! traitress to thy friends! How hast thou ruined me! May Zeus, my ancestor, smite thee with his fiery bolt and uproot thee from thy place. Did I not foresee thy purpose, did I not bid thee keep silence on the very matter which is now my shame? But thou wouldst not be still; wherefore my fair name will not go with me to the tomb. But now I must another scheme devise. Yon youth, in the keenness of his fury, will tell his father of my sin, and the aged Pittheus of my state, and fill the world with stories to my shame. Perdition seize thee and every meddling fool who by dishonest means would serve unwilling friends!

NUR. Mistress, thou may'st condemn the mischief I have done, for sorrow's sting o'ermasters thy judgment; yet can I answer thee in face of this, if thou wilt hear. 'Twas I who nurtured thee; I love thee still; but in my search for medicine to cure thy sickness I found what least I sought. Had I but succeeded, I had been counted wise, for the credit we get for wisdom is measured by our success.

PHÆ. Is it just, is it any satisfaction to me, that thou shouldst wound me first, then bandy words with me?

NUR. We dwell on this too long; I was not wise, I own; but there are yet ways of escape from the trouble, my child.

PHÆ. Be dumb henceforth; evil was thy first advice to me, evil too thy attempted scheme. Begone and leave me, look to thyself; I will my own fortunes for the best arrange. [*Exit* NURSE.] Ye noble daughters of Trœzen, grant me the only boon I crave; in silence bury what ye here have heard.

CHO. By majestic Artemis, child of Zeus, I swear I will never divulge aught of thy sorrows.

1ST HALF CHO.   Friends, what shall we do? think you we should enter the house, and loose the queen from the tight-drawn noose?

2ND HALF CHO.   Why should *we*? Are there not young servants here? To do too much is not a safe course in life.

MES.   Lay out the hapless corpse, straighten the limbs. This was a bitter way to sit at home and keep my master's house!

[*Exit* MESSENGER.

CHO.   She is dead, poor lady, so I hear. Already are they laying out the corpse.

THE.   Ladies, can ye tell me what the uproar in the palace means? There came the sound of servants weeping bitterly to mine ear. None of my household deign to open wide the gates and give me glad welcome as a traveller from prophetic shrines. Hath aught befallen old Pittheus? No. Though he be well advanced in years, yet should I mourn, were he to quit this house.

CHO.   'Tis not against the old, Theseus, that fate, to strike thee, aims this blow; prepare thy sorrow for a younger corpse.

THE.   Woe is me! is it a child's life death robs me of?

CHO.   They live; but, cruellest news of all for thee, their mother is no more.

THE.   What! my wife dead? By what cruel mischance?

CHO.   About her neck she tied the hangman's knot.

THE.   Had grief so chilled her blood? or what had befallen her?

CHO.   I know but this, for I am myself but now arrived at the house to mourn thy sorrows, O Theseus.

THE.   Woe is me! why have I crowned my head with woven garlands, when misfortune greets my embassage? Unbolt the doors, servants, loose their fastenings, that I may see the piteous sight, my wife, whose death is death to me.

[*The palace opens, disclosing the corpse.*]

CHO.   Woe! woe is thee for thy piteous lot! thou hast done thyself a hurt deep enough to overthrow this family. Ah! ah! the daring of it! done to death by violence and unnatural means, the desperate effort of thy own poor hand! Who cast the shadow o'er thy life, poor lady?

THE.   Ah me, my cruel lot! sorrow hath done her worst on me. O fortune, how heavily hast thou set thy foot on me and on my house, by fiendish hands inflicting an unexpected stain? Nay, 'tis complete effacement of my life, making it impossible; for I see, alas! so wide an ocean of grief that I can never swim to shore again, nor breast the tide of this calamity. How shall I speak of thee, my poor wife, what tale of direst suffering tell? Thou art vanished like a bird from the covert of my hand, taking one headlong leap from me to Hades' halls. Alas, and woe! this is a bitter, bitter sight! This must be a judgment sent by God for the sins of an ancestor, which from some far source I am bringing on myself.

CHO.   My prince, 'tis not to thee alone such sorrows come; thou hast lost a noble wife, but so have many others.

THE.   Fain would I go hide me 'neath earth's blackest depth, to dwell in darkness with the dead in misery, now that I am reft of thy dear presence! for thou hast slain me than thyself e'en more. Who can tell me what caused the fatal stroke that reached thy heart, dear wife? Will no one tell me what befell? doth my palace all in vain give shelter to a herd of menials? Woe, woe for thee, my wife! sorrows past speech, past bearing, I behold within my house; myself a ruined man, my home a solitude, my children orphans!

CHO.   Gone and left us hast thou, fondest wife and noblest of all women 'neath the sun's bright eye or night's star-lit radiance. Poor house, what sorrows are thy portion now! My eyes are wet with streams of tears to see thy fate; but the sequel to this tragedy has long with terror filled me.

THE.   Ha! what means this letter? clasped in her dear hand it hath some strange tale to tell. Hath she, poor lady, as a last request, written her bidding as to my marriage and her children? Take heart, poor ghost; no wife henceforth shall wed thy Theseus or invade his house. Ah! how yon seal of my dead wife stamped with her golden ring affects my sight! Come, I will unfold the sealed packet and read her letter's message to me.

CHO.   Woe unto us! Here is yet another evil in the train by heaven sent. Looking to what has happened, I should count my lot in life no longer worth one's while to gain. My master's house, alas! is ruined, brought to naught, I say. Spare it, O Heaven, if it may be. Hearken to my prayer, for I see, as with prophetic eye, an omen boding mischief.

THE.   O horror! woe on woe! and still they come, too deep for words, too heavy to bear. Ah me!

CHO.   What is it? speak, if I may share in it.

THO.   This letter loudly tells a hideous tale! where can I escape my load of woe? For I am ruined and undone, so awful are the words I find here written clear as if she cried them to me; woe is me!

CHO.   Alas! thy words declare themselves the harbingers of woe.

THE.   I can no longer keep the cursed tale within the portal of my lips, cruel though its utterance be. Ah me! Hippolytus hath dared by brutal force to violate my honour, recking naught of Zeus, whose awful eye is over all. O father Poseidon, once didst thou promise

to fulfil three prayers of mine; answer one of these and slay my
son, let him not escape this single day, if the prayers thou gavest
me were indeed with issue fraught.

CHO. O king, I do conjure thee, call back that prayer; hereafter thou
wilt know thy error. Hear, I pray.

THE. Impossible! Moreover I will banish him from this land, and by
one of two fates shall he be struck down; either Poseidon, out of
respect to my prayer, will cast his dead body into the house of
Hades; or exiled from this land, a wanderer to some foreign shore,
shall he eke out a life of misery.

CHO. Lo! where himself doth come, thy son Hippolytus, in good
time; dismiss thy hurtful rage, King Theseus, and bethink thee
what is best for thy family.

HIP. I heard thy voice, father, and hasted to come hither; yet know I
not the cause of thy present sorrow, but would fain learn of thee.
Ha! what is this? thy wife a corpse I see; this is passing strange;
'twas but now I left her; a moment since she looked upon the
light. How came she thus? the manner of her death? this would I
learn of thee, father. Art dumb? silence availeth not in trouble;
nay, for the heart that fain would know all must show its curiosity
even in sorrow's hour. Be sure it is not right, father, to hide misfortunes from those who love, ay, more than love thee.

THE. O ye sons of men, victims of a thousand idle errors, why teach
your countless crafts, why scheme and seek to find a way for every-
thing, while one thing ye know not nor ever yet have made your
prize, a way to teach them wisdom whose souls are void of sense?

HIP. A very master in his craft the man, who can force fools to be
wise! But these ill-timed subtleties of thine, father, make me fear
thy tongue is running riot through trouble.

THE. Fie upon thee! man needs should have some certain test set up
to try his friends, some touchstone of their hearts, to know each
friend whether he be true or false; all men should have two voices,
one the voice of honesty, expediency's the other, so would honesty
confute its knavish opposite, and then we could not be deceived.

HIP. Say, hath some friend been slandering me and hath he still thine
ear? am I, though guiltless, banned? I am amazed indeed; thy random, frantic words fill me with wild alarm.

THE. O the mind of mortal man! to what lengths will it proceed?
What limit will its bold assurance have? for if it goes on growing
as man's life advances, and each successor outdo the man before
him in villainy, the gods will have to add another sphere unto the
world, which shall take in the knaves and villains. Behold this
man; he, my own son, hath outraged mine honour, his guilt most

clearly proved by my dead wife. Now, since thou hast dared this
loathly crime, come, look thy father in the face. Art thou the man
who dost with gods consort, as one above the vulgar herd? art thou
the chaste and sinless saint? Thy boasts will never persuade me to
be guilty of attributing ignorance to gods. Go then, vaunt thyself,
and drive thy petty trade in viands formed of lifeless food; take
Orpheus for thy chief and go a-revelling, with all honour for the
vapourings of many a written scroll, seeing thou now art caught.
Let all beware, I say, of such hypocrites! who hunt their prey with
fine words, and all the while are scheming villainy. She is dead;
dost think that this will save thee? Why this convicts thee more
than all, abandoned wretch! What oaths, what pleas can outweigh
this letter, so that thou shouldst 'scape thy doom? Thou wilt assert
she hated thee, that 'twixt the bastard and the true-born child nature has herself put war; it seems then by thy showing she made a
sorry bargain with her life, if to gratify her hate of thee she lost
what most she prized. 'Tis said, no doubt, that frailty finds no
place in man but is innate in woman; my experience is, young
men are no more secure than women, whenso the Queen of Love
excites a youthful breast; although their sex comes in to help
them. Yet why do I thus bandy words with thee, when before me
lies the corpse, to be the clearest witness? Begone at once, an exile
from this land, and ne'er set foot again in god-built Athens nor in
the confines of my dominion. For if I am tamely to submit to this
treatment from such as thee, no more will Sinis, robber of the
Isthmus, bear me witness how I slew him, but say my boasts are
idle, nor will those rocks Scironian, that fringe the sea, call me the
miscreants' scourge.

CHO.   I know not how to call happy any child of man; for that which
was first has turned and now is last.

HIP.   Father, thy wrath and the tension of thy mind are terrible; yet
this charge, specious though its arguments appear, becomes a
calumny, if one lay it bare. Small skill have I in speaking to a
crowd, but have a readier wit for comrades of mine own age and
small companies. Yea, and this is as it should be; for they, whom
the wise despise, are better qualified to speak before a mob. Yet am
I constrained under the present circumstances to break silence.
And at the outset will I take the point which formed the basis of
thy stealthy attack on me, designed to put me out of court unheard; dost see yon sun, this earth? These do not contain, for all
thou dost deny it, chastity surpassing mine. To reverence God I
count the highest knowledge, and to adopt as friends not those
who attempt injustice, but such as would blush to propose to their

companions aught disgraceful or pleasure them by shameful services; to mock at friends is not my way, father, but I am still the same behind their backs as to their face. The very crime thou thinkest to catch me in, is just the one I am untainted with, for to this day have I kept me pure from women. Nor know I aught thereof, save what I hear or see in pictures, for I have no wish to look even on these, so pure my virgin soul. I grant my claim to chastity may not convince thee; well, 'tis then for thee to show the way I was corrupted. Did this woman exceed in beauty all her sex? Did I aspire to fill the husband's place after thee and succeed to thy house? [That surely would have made me out a fool, a creature void of sense. Thou wilt say, "Your chaste man loves to lord it." No, no! say I, sovereignty pleases only those whose hearts are quite corrupt. Now, I would be the first and best at all the games in Hellas, but second in the state, for ever happy thus with the noblest for my friends. For there one may be happy, and the absence of danger gives a charm beyond all princely joys.] One thing I have not said, the rest thou hast. Had I a witness to attest my purity, and were I pitted 'gainst her still alive, facts would show thee on enquiry who the culprit was. Now by Zeus, the god of oaths, and by the earth, whereon we stand, I swear to thee I never did lay hand upon thy wife nor would have wished to, or have harboured such a thought. Slay me, ye gods! rob me of name and honour, from home and city cast me forth, a wandering exile o'er the earth! nor sea nor land receive my bones when I am dead, if I am such a miscreant! I cannot say if she through fear destroyed herself, for more than this am I forbid. With her discretion took the place of chastity, while I, though chaste, was not discreet in using this virtue.

CHO. Thy oath by heaven, strong security, sufficiently refutes the charge.

THE. A wizard or magician must the fellow be, to think he can first flout me, his father, then by coolness master my resolve.

HIP. Father, thy part in this doth fill me with amaze; wert thou my son and I thy sire, by heaven! I would have slain, not let thee off with banishment, hadst thou presumed to violate my honour.

THE. A just remark! yet shalt thou not die by the sentence thine own lips pronounce upon thyself; for death, that cometh in a moment, is an easy end for wretchedness. Nay, thou shalt be exiled from thy fatherland, [and wandering to a foreign shore drag out a life of misery; for such are the wages of sin.]

HIP. Oh! what wilt thou do? Wilt thou banish me, without so much as waiting for Time's evidence on my case?

THE.   Ay, beyond the sea, beyond the bounds of Atlas, if I could, so deeply do I hate thee.

HIP.   What! banish me untried, without even testing my oath, the pledge I offer, or the voice of seers?

THE.   This letter here, though it bears no seers' signs, arraigns thy pledges; as for birds that fly o'er our heads, a long farewell to them.

HIP. [*aside.*]   Great gods! why do I not unlock my lips, seeing that I am ruined by you, the objects of my reverence? No, I will not; I should nowise persuade those whom I ought to, and in vain should break the oath I swore.

THE.   Fie upon thee! that solemn air of thine is more than I can bear. Begone from thy native land forthwith!

HIP.   Whither shall I turn? Ah me! whose friendly house will take me in, an exile on so grave a charge?

THE.   Seek one who loves to entertain as guests and partners in his crimes corrupters of men's wives.

HIP.   Ah me! this wounds my heart and brings me nigh to tears to think that I should appear so vile, and thou believe me so.

THE.   Thy tears and forethought had been more in season when thou didst presume to outrage thy father's wife.

HIP.   O house, I would thou couldst speak for me and witness if I am so vile!

THE.   Dost fly to speechless witnesses? This deed, though it speaketh not, proves thy guilt clearly.

HIP.   Alas! Would I could stand and face myself, so should I weep to see the sorrows I endure.

THE.   Ay, 'tis thy character to honour thyself far more than reverence thy parents, as thou shouldst.

HIP.   Unhappy mother! son of sorrow! Heaven keep all friends of mine from bastard birth!

THE.   Ho! servants, drag him hence! You heard my proclamation long ago condemning him to exile.

HIP.   Whoso of them doth lay a hand on me shall rue it; thyself expel me, if thy spirit move thee, from the land.

THE.   I will, unless my word thou straight obey; no pity for thy exile steals into my heart.   [*Exit* THESEUS.

HIP.   The sentence then, it seems, is passed. Ah, misery! How well I know the truth herein, but know no way to tell it! O daughter of Latona, dearest to me of all deities, partner, comrade in the chase, far from glorious Athens must I fly. Farewell, city and land of Erechtheus; farewell, Trœzen, most joyous home wherein to pass the spring of life; 'tis my last sight of thee, farewell! Come, my comrades in this land, young like me, greet me kindly and escort

me forth, for never will ye behold a purer soul, for all my father's
doubts.   [*Exit* HIPPOLYTUS.

CHO.   In very deed the thoughts I have about the gods, whenso they
come into my mind, do much to soothe its grief, but though I
cherish secret hopes of some great guiding will, yet am I at fault
when I survey the fate and doings of the sons of men; change suc-
ceeds to change, and man's life veers and shifts in endless rest-
lessness. Fortune grant me this, I pray, at heaven's hand,—a happy
lot in life and a soul from sorrow free; opinions let me hold not too
precise nor yet too hollow; but, lightly changing my habits to each
morrow as it comes, may I thus attain a life of bliss! For now no
more is my mind free from doubts, unlooked-for sights greet my
vision; for lo! I see the morning star of Athens, eye of Hellas, driven by his father's fury to another land. Mourn, ye sands of my native shores, ye oak-groves on the hills, where with his fleet hounds
he would hunt the quarry to the death, attending on Dictynna,
awful queen. No more will he mount his car drawn by Venetian
steeds, filling the course round Limna with the prancing of his
trained horses. Nevermore in his father's house shall he wake the
Muse that never slept beneath his lute-strings; no hand will crown
the spots where rests the maiden Latona 'mid the boskage deep;
nor evermore shall our virgins vie to win thy love, now thou art
banished; while I with tears at thy unhappy fate shall endure a lot
all undeserved. Ah! hapless mother, in vain didst thou bring forth,
it seems. I am angered with the gods; out upon them! O ye linkèd
Graces, why are ye sending from his native land this poor youth, a
guiltless sufferer, far from his home?

But lo! I see a servant of Hippolytus hasting with troubled looks
towards the palace.

2ND MES.   Ladies, where may I find Theseus, king of the country?
pray, tell me if ye know; is he within the palace here?

CHO.   Lo! himself approaches from the palace.

2ND MES.   Theseus, I am the bearer of troublous tidings to thee and
all citizens who dwell in Athens or the bounds of Trœzen.

THE.   How now? hath some strange calamity o'ertaken these two
neighbouring cities?

2ND MES.   In one brief word, Hippolytus is dead. 'Tis true one slen-
der thread still links him to the light of life.

THE.   Who slew him? Did some husband come to blows with him,
one whose wife, like mine, had suffered brutal violence?

2ND MES.   He perished through those steeds that drew his chariot,
and through the curses thou didst utter, praying to thy sire, the
ocean-king, to slay thy son.

THE. Ye gods and king Poseidon, thou hast proved my parentage by hearkening to my prayer! Say how he perished; how fell the uplifted hand of Justice to smite the villain who dishonoured me?

2ND MES. Hard by the wave-beat shore were we combing out his horses' manes, weeping the while, for one had come to say that Hippolytus was harshly exiled by thee and nevermore would return to set foot in this land. Then came he, telling the same doleful tale to us upon the beach, and with him was a countless throng of friends who followed after. At length he stayed his lamentation and spake: "Why weakly rave on this wise? My father's commands must be obeyed. Ho! servants, harness my horses to the chariot; this is no longer now city of mine. Thereupon each one of us bestirred himself, and, ere a man could say 'twas done, we had the horses standing ready at our master's side. Then he caught up the reins from the chariot-rail, first fitting his feet exactly in the hollows made for them. But first with outspread palms he called upon the gods, "O Zeus, now strike me dead, if I have sinned, and let my father learn how he is wronging me, in death at least, if not in life." Therewith he seized the whip and lashed each horse in turn; while we, close by his chariot, near the reins, kept up with him along the road that leads direct to Argos and Epidaurus. And just as we were coming to a desert spot, a strip of sand beyond the borders of this country, sloping right to the Saronic gulf, there issued thence a deep rumbling sound, as it were an earthquake, a fearsome noise, and the horses reared their heads and pricked their ears, while we were filled with wild alarm to know whence came the sound; when, as we gazed toward the wave-beat shore, a wave tremendous we beheld towering to the skies, so that from our view the cliffs of Sciron vanished, for it hid the isthmus and the rock of Asclepius; then swelling and frothing with a crest of foam, the sea discharged it toward the beach where stood the harnessed car, and in the moment that it broke, that mighty wall of waters, there issued from the wave a monstrous bull, whose bellowing filled the land with fearsome echoes, a sight too awful as it seemed to us who witnessed it. A panic seized the horses there and then, but our master, to horses' ways quite used, gripped in both hands his reins, and tying them to his body pulled them backward as the sailor pulls his oar; but the horses gnashed the forged bits between their teeth and bore him wildly on, regardless of their master's guiding hand or rein or jointed car. And oft as he would take the guiding rein and steer for softer ground, showed that bull in front to turn him back again, maddening his team with terror; but if in their frantic career they ran towards the rocks, he would draw nigh the chariot-rail, keeping up with them, until, suddenly dashing the wheel against a stone, he upset and wrecked the car; then was dire confusion, axle-boxes and linch-pins springing into the air. While he, poor youth, entangled in the reins was dragged along, bound by a stubborn knot, his poor head dashed against the rocks, his flesh all torn, the while he cried out piteously, "Stay, stay, my horses whom my own hand hath fed at the manger, destroy me not utterly. O luckless curse of a father! Will no one come and save me for all my virtue?" Now we, though much we longed to help, were left far behind. At last, I know not how, he broke loose from the shapely reins that bound him, a faint breath of life still in him; but the horses disappeared, and that portentous bull, among the rocky ground, I know not where. I am but a slave in thy house, 'tis true, O king, yet will I never believe so monstrous a charge against thy son's character, no! not though the whole race of womankind should hang itself, or one should fill with writing every pine-tree tablet grown in Ida, sure as I am of his uprightness.

CHO.   Alas! new troubles come to plague us, nor is there any escape from fate and necessity.

THE.   My hatred for him who hath thus suffered made me glad at thy tidings, yet from regard for the gods and him, because he is my son, I feel neither joy nor sorrow at his sufferings.

2ND MES.   But say, are we to bring the victim hither, or how are we to fulfil thy wishes? Bethink thee; if by me thou wilt be schooled, thou wilt not harshly treat thy son in his sad plight.

THE.   Bring him hither, that when I see him face to face, who hath denied having polluted my wife's honour, I may by words and heaven's visitation convict him.

CHO.   Ah! Cypris, thine the hand that guides the stubborn hearts of gods and men; thine, and that attendant boy's, who, with painted plumage gay, flutters round his victims on lightning wing. O'er the land and booming deep on golden pinion borne flits the god of Love, maddening the heart and beguiling the senses of all whom he attacks, savage whelps on mountains bred, ocean's monsters, creatures of this sun-warmed earth, and man; thine, O Cypris, thine alone the sovereign power to rule them all.

ART.   Hearken, I bid thee, noble son of Ægeus: lo! 'tis I, Latona's child, that speak, I, Artemis. Why, Theseus, to thy sorrow dost thou rejoice at these tidings, seeing that thou hast slain thy son most impiously, listening to a charge not clearly proved, but falsely sworn to by thy wife? though clearly has the curse therefrom upon thee fallen. Why dost thou not for very shame hide beneath the dark places of the earth, or change thy human life and soar on wings to escape this tribulation? 'Mongst men of honour thou hast now no share in life. Hearken, Theseus; I will put thy wretched case. Yet will it naught avail thee, if I do, but vex thy heart; still with this intent I came, to show thy son's pure heart,—that he may die with honour,—as well the frenzy, and, in a sense, the nobleness of thy wife; for she was cruelly stung with a passion for thy son by that goddess whom all we, that joy in virgin purity, detest. And though she strove to conquer love by resolution, yet by no fault of hers she fell, thanks to her nurse's strategy, who did reveal her malady unto thy son under oath. But he would none of her counsels, as indeed was right, nor yet, when thou didst revile him, would he break the oath he swore, from piety. She meantime, fearful of being found out, wrote a lying letter, destroying by guile thy son, but yet persuading thee.

THE.   Woe is me!

ART.   Doth my story wound thee, Theseus? Be still awhile; hear what follows, so wilt thou have more cause to groan. Dost remember those three prayers thy father granted thee, fraught with certain issue? 'Tis one of these thou hast misused, unnatural wretch, against thy son, instead of aiming it at an enemy. Thy sea-god sire, 'tis true, for all his kind intent, hath granted that boon he was compelled, by reason of his promise, to grant. But thou alike in his eyes and in mine hast shewn thy evil heart, in that thou hast forestalled all proof or voice prophetic, hast made no inquiry, nor taken time for consideration, but with undue haste cursed thy son even to the death.

THE.   Perdition seize me! Queen revered!

ART.   An awful deed was thine, but still even for this thou mayest obtain pardon; for it was Cypris that would have it so, sating the fury of her soul. For this is law amongst us gods; none of us will thwart his neighbour's will, but ever we stand aloof. For be well assured, did I not fear Zeus, never would I have incurred the bitter shame of handing over to death a man of all his kind to me most dear. As for thy sin, first thy ignorance absolves thee from its villainy, next thy wife, who is dead, was lavish in her use of convincing arguments to influence thy mind. On thee in chief this storm of woe hath burst, yet is it some grief to me as well; for when the righteous die, there is no joy in heaven, albeit we try to destroy the wicked, house and home.

CHO.   Lo! where he comes, this hapless youth, his fair young flesh and auburn locks most shamefully handled. Unhappy house! what twofold sorrow doth o'ertake its halls, through heaven's ordinance!

HIP.   Ah! ah! woe is me! foully undone by an impious father's impious imprecation! Undone, undone! woe is me! Through my head shoot fearful pains; my brain throbs convulsively. Stop, let me rest my worn-out frame. Oh, oh! Accursed steeds, that mine own hand did feed, ye have been my ruin and my death. O by the gods, good sirs, I beseech ye, softly touch my wounded limbs. Who stands there at my right side? Lift me tenderly; with slow and even step conduct a poor wretch cursed by his mistaken sire. Great Zeus, dost thou see this? Me thy reverent worshipper, me who left all men behind in purity, plunged thus into yawning Hades 'neath the earth, reft of life; in vain the toils I have endured through my piety towards mankind. Ah me! ah me! O the thrill of anguish shooting through me! Set me down, poor wretch I am; come Death to set me free! Kill me, end my sufferings. O for a sword two-edged to hack my flesh, and close this mortal life! Ill-fated curse of my father! the crimes of bloody kinsmen, ancestors of old, now pass their boundaries and tarry not, and upon me are they come all guiltless as I am; ah! why? Alas, alas! what can I say? How from my life get rid of this relentless agony? O that the stern Death-god, night's black visitant, would give my sufferings rest!

ART.   Poor sufferer! cruel the fate that links thee to it! Thy noble soul hath been thy ruin.

HIP.   Ah! the fragrance from my goddess wafted! Even in my agony I feel thee near and find relief; she is here in this very place, my goddess Artemis.

ART.   She is, poor sufferer! the goddess thou hast loved the best.

HIP.   Dost see me, mistress mine? dost see my present suffering?

ART.   I see thee, but mine eyes no tear may weep.

HIP.   Thou hast none now to lead the hunt or tend thy fane.

ART.   None now; yet e'en in death I love thee still.

HIP.   None to groom thy steeds, or guard thy shrines.

ART.   'Twas Cypris, mistress of iniquity, devised this evil.

HIP.   Ah me! now know I the goddess who destroyed me.

ART.   She was jealous of her slighted honour, vexed at thy chaste life.

HIP.   Ah! then I see her single hand hath struck down three of us.

ART.   Thy sire and thee, and last thy father's wife.

HIP.   My sire's ill-luck as well as mine I mourn.

ART.   He was deceived by a goddess's design.

HIP.   Woe is thee, my father, in this sad mischance!

THE.   My son, I am a ruined man; life has no joys for me.

HIP.   For this mistake I mourn thee rather than myself.

THE.   O that I had died for thee, my son!

HIP.   Ah! those fatal gifts thy sire Poseidon gave.

THE.   Would God these lips had never uttered that prayer!

HIP.   Why not? thou wouldst in any case have slain me in thy fury then.

THE.   Yes; Heaven had perverted my power to think.

HIP.   O that the race of men could bring a curse upon the gods!

ART.   Enough! for though thou pass to gloom beneath the earth, the wrath of Cypris shall not, at her will, fall on thee unrequited, because thou hadst a noble righteous soul. For I with mine own hand will with these unerring shafts avenge me on another, who is her votary, dearest to her of all the sons of men. And to thee, poor sufferer, for thy anguish now will I grant high honours in the city of Trœzen; for thee shall maids unwed before their marriage cut off their hair, thy harvest through the long roll of time of countless bitter tears. Yea, and for ever shall the virgin choir hymn thy sad memory, nor shall Phædra's love for thee fall into oblivion and pass away unnoticed. But thou, O son of old Ægeus, take thy son in thine arms, draw him close to thee, for unwittingly thou slewest him, and men may well commit an error when gods put it in their way. And thee Hippolytus, I admonish; hate not thy sire, for in this death thou dost but meet thy destined fate. And now farewell! 'tis not for me to gaze upon the dead, or pollute my sight with death-scenes, and e'en now I see thee nigh that evil moment.

[*Exit* ARTEMIS.

HIP.   Farewell, blest virgin queen! leave me now! How easily thou resignest our long friendship! I am reconciled with my father at thy desire, yea, for ever before I would obey thy bidding. Ah me! the darkness is settling even now upon my eyes. Take me, father, in thy arms, lift me up.

THE.   Woe is me, my son! what art thou doing to me thy hapless sire!

HIP.   I am a broken man; yes, I see the gates that close upon the dead.

THE.   Canst leave me thus with murder on my soul!

HIP.   No, no; I set thee free from this bloodguiltiness.

THE.   What sayest thou? dost absolve me from bloodshed?

HIP.   Artemis, the archer-queen, is my witness that I do.

THE.   My own dear child, how generous dost thou show thyself to thy father!

HIP.   Farewell, dear father! a long farewell to thee!

THE.   O that holy, noble soul of thine!

HIP.   Pray to have children such as me born in lawful wedlock.

THE.   O leave me not, my son; endure awhile.

HIP.   'Tis finished, my endurance; I die, father; quickly cover my face with a mantle.

THE.   O glorious Athens, realm of Pallas, what a splendid hero ye have lost! Ah me, ah me! How oft shall I remember thy evil work, O Cypris!

CHO. On all our citizens hath come this universal sorrow, unforeseen. Now shall the copious tear gush forth, for sad news about great men takes more than usual hold upon the heart.

DOVER · THRIFT · EDITIONS

PLAYS

LIFE IS A DREAM, Pedro Calderón de la Barca. 96pp. 0-486-42124-4
H. M. S. PINAFORE, William Schwenck Gilbert. 64pp. 0-486-41114-1
THE MIKADO, William Schwenck Gilbert. 64pp. 0-486-27268-0
SHE STOOPS TO CONQUER, Oliver Goldsmith. 80pp. 0-486-26867-5
THE LOWER DEPTHS, Maxim Gorky. 80pp. 0-486-41115-X
A DOLL'S HOUSE, Henrik Ibsen. 80pp. 0-486-27062-9
GHOSTS, Henrik Ibsen. 64pp. 0-486-29852-3
HEDDA GABLER, Henrik Ibsen. 80pp. 0-486-26469-6
PEER GYNT, Henrik Ibsen. 144pp. 0-486-42686-6
THE WILD DUCK, Henrik Ibsen. 96pp. 0-486-41116-8
VOLPONE, Ben Jonson. 112pp. 0-486-28049-7
DR. FAUSTUS, Christopher Marlowe. 64pp. 0-486-28208-2
TAMBURLAINE, Christopher Marlowe. 128pp. 0-486-42125-2
THE IMAGINARY INVALID, Molière. 96pp. 0-486-43789-2
THE MISANTHROPE, Molière. 64pp. 0-486-27065-3
RIGHT YOU ARE, IF YOU THINK YOU ARE, Luigi Pirandello. 64pp. (Not available in Europe or United Kingdom.) 0-486-29576-1
SIX CHARACTERS IN SEARCH OF AN AUTHOR, Luigi Pirandello. 64pp. (Not available in Europe or United Kingdom.) 0-486-29992-9
PHÈDRE, Jean Racine. 64pp. 0-486-41927-4
HANDS AROUND, Arthur Schnitzler. 64pp. 0-486-28724-6
ANTONY AND CLEOPATRA, William Shakespeare. 128pp. 0-486-40062-X
AS YOU LIKE IT, William Shakespeare. 80pp. 0-486-40432-3
HAMLET, William Shakespeare. 128pp. 0-486-27278-8
HENRY IV, William Shakespeare. 96pp. 0-486-29584-2
JULIUS CAESAR, William Shakespeare. 80pp. 0-486-26876-4
KING LEAR, William Shakespeare. 112pp. 0-486-28058-6
LOVE'S LABOUR'S LOST, William Shakespeare. 64pp. 0-486-41929-0
MACBETH, William Shakespeare. 96pp. 0-486-27802-6
MEASURE FOR MEASURE, William Shakespeare. 96pp. 0-486-40889-2
THE MERCHANT OF VENICE, William Shakespeare. 96pp. 0-486-28492-1
A MIDSUMMER NIGHT'S DREAM, William Shakespeare. 80pp. 0-486-27067-X
MUCH ADO ABOUT NOTHING, William Shakespeare. 80pp. 0-486-28272-4
OTHELLO, William Shakespeare. 112pp. 0-486-29097-2
RICHARD III, William Shakespeare. 112pp. 0-486-28747-5
ROMEO AND JULIET, William Shakespeare. 96pp. 0-486-27557-4
THE TAMING OF THE SHREW, William Shakespeare. 96pp. 0-486-29765-9
THE TEMPEST, William Shakespeare. 96pp. 0-486-40658-X
TWELFTH NIGHT; OR, WHAT YOU WILL, William Shakespeare. 80pp. 0-486-29290-8
ARMS AND THE MAN, George Bernard Shaw. 80pp. (Not available in Europe or United Kingdom.) 0-486-26476-9
HEARTBREAK HOUSE, George Bernard Shaw. 128pp. (Not available in Europe or United Kingdom.) 0-486-29291-6
PYGMALION, George Bernard Shaw. 96pp. (Available in U.S. only.) 0-486-28222-8
THE RIVALS, Richard Brinsley Sheridan. 96pp. 0-486-40433-1
THE SCHOOL FOR SCANDAL, Richard Brinsley Sheridan. 96pp. 0-486-26687-7
ANTIGONE, Sophocles. 64pp. 0-486-27804-2
OEDIPUS AT COLONUS, Sophocles. 64pp. 0-486-40659-8
OEDIPUS REX, Sophocles. 64pp. 0-486-26877-2